Modie

 AND

The Power of
the BellKeys

Stefanie Bailey

and

C.J. Bailey

Book design by The Floating Gallery
www.thefloatinggallery.com

Printed in the United States of America

Modie and the Power of the BellKeys
Copyright © 2004 by Stefanie Bailey and C.J. Bailey

Library of Congress Control Number 2004114847
ISBN 0-9762502-0-9

If you want your children to be intelligent,
read them fairy tales. If you want them to be
more intelligent, read them more fairy tales.

Albert Einstein

For Grace — Perfect name for a perfect name — I so enjoy having you — smile! Always use your imagination. Stefanie Ridley

The Modie Series is lovingly dedicated to our grandmother
FLORA "MAXINE" BAILEY
(1921–2003)

When I least expected it—inspiration was found!

With special thanks—filled with hugs and kisses to our children
Shayla
Jonas
Jessica
Rebecca
Drew
Kara
Bailey
Hannah
Maxim

Prologue

The stars fell from the night sky. Hearing their cries, the Regent knew that the time had come.

With a sense of purpose, he climbed the stone steps through the turret, which led to a catwalk high above his castle. There stood a magnificent structure known as the Solarium, made entirely of glass and featured a closed tulip-shaped roof. A fine gold mist containing the Royal Draugs surrounded the Regent's body, protecting him from any direct visual threat. His long, stark white beard with a jet-black streak running down the middle, swished back and forth brushing against his blue monk-like robe. Once he reached the top, he saw the golden starcatcher, fashioned like a fishing pole. The starcatcher was the answer to the future.

The six Ancient Ones, the most trusted men of his world, acknowledged the Regent's presence by standing at attention in a single file with their backs to the Solarium.

"Everything is ready, sire, just as you requested," said Rasoz, the oldest of the six, as he bowed.

"Then it shall be done. May the path be one of a pure heart," said the Regent as his antennae twitched with anticipation. Bending down, he clasped the sparkling gold starcatcher in his hand. He raised it high for a split second, then brought it down hard on the stone floor.

"Protect!" he yelled.

Instantly, the starcatcher vibrated and hummed. The golden rod came to life at the Regent's command. Swiftly, he then brought his focus to the star-littered sky. He cast the line with a diligent, smooth motion. A wisp of silver flew out searching for its intended prize. With a flick of the wrist, the Regent guided the line to a distant falling star. A net opened, capturing the small ball of power. Rapidly, he reeled in, feeling the strain from the weight. Three more times he cast and reeled, completing the task of capturing four stars.

Once all were placed safely in a satchel tied to his waist, the Ancient Ones opened the glass doors to the Solarium, which was especially made to house the newest additions. With a formal bow, all six beckoned the Regent in.

Right below the glass-peaked roof stood four antique pillars that formed a square. In the center was a larger pillar etched in gold that will remain vacant and untouched—waiting for the time of the New Kingdom to be ruled by the chosen.

The Regent placed each star on a pillar—their new home. Upon contact, the stars glowed bright speaking of the individual gift they each possessed—an offering as a sign of gratitude for catching them before they completely fell.

At that moment, the stars became special realms created for the Regent to guide: The Pilutars, the favorite of the Regent for they were made in his likeness, lived in a meadow outside of LaHiere Village. They were gifted with a strong affinity with Natural Earth's structures where they could manipulate the trees, earth and mountains. Second came the Drazils, who resided in the desert lands. They are changelings that could take on any form. The Skylars, the third realm, were bestowed with the ability to work with Natural Earth's forces such as wind and rain. Because they lived in the clouds and forests, their ability to light-skim was a blessing so they could travel rapidly between areas. The Gilfins, the last realm, lived in the bodies of water within and underneath Natural Earth. All four realms were considered the authority over other mystical, magical beings while all were ruled by the Regent.

All creatures had the gift of choice to decide whether to walk in the path for good or for evil. Because they could choose, evil became rampant within the realms. Several species became greedy with their gifts and wanted more. Those few who chose this path in life were sent through the Banishing Door, a prison that was created for them to live out the rest of their time.

CHAPTER 1

The Legend

The Regent stood on the catwalk like he had hundreds of times before. Hearing a slight sound behind him, he turned and his face broke into a large smile. His daughter, Flora, with bare feet and in a long, white nightgown and her tiny bell necklace that gleamed in the starlight, approached him with two starcatchers in her hands. One was his, the larger of the two; the other a special gift for her birthday from the Ancient Ones.

The Regent got down on his knees so that he would be on Flora's level and took his starcatcher from her. His eyes searched her young face as he wondered if she was truly ready to start what had been fated, because in all honesty he was just not ready to let her grow up so soon.

"I thought I heard the stars crying out—is it time, Daddy?" Flora asked in a reverent whisper.

"Yes, poppet, it is. But, wouldn't you like to take a few more weeks of training? The Ancient Ones said you are ready, but we can always wait until later. There will always be another night with stars falling."

Flora tilted her head, making her long curly blonde hair brush against her waist. Her ice-blue eyes sparkled with love as she realized this was another of her father's stall tactics. She clasped her starcatcher closer to her and straightened her back making her slightly grown antennae stand proud. It was time to let her father know that she was grown up and ready to face her future. Flora clamped her lips closed with determination and opened her mind the way the Ancient Ones have been teaching her.

"There may be another night of stars falling."

Startled, the Regent looked at his daughter with amazement! She had learned the exclusive gift for a destined Oracle and Regent. She was talking to him in his mind!

Flora continued to concentrate. "But this is the night that MY star is falling. I can feel it, Daddy. I have studied the starcatcher and its technique for well over a year, you know. I think, no wait! I *believe* that I am ready." She opened her eyes and looked at her father with expectation.

"I see that the Ancients have been busy," he said dryly.

"Were you surprised? I have been working so hard on sending my thoughts, you know. You should have seen Uncle Rasoz's face when I did it to him for real! So, can I, Daddy? Can I catch my star now?"

The Regent got up and stood over his daughter. With a heavy sigh, he ran a hand over his face then stroked his long beard whose black streak now had some gray.

"So, be it. You may begin." Sweeping his arm out, he beckoned Flora to approach the outer wall.

She walked forward with anticipation, then glanced back. "You need to stand back. I need to concentrate, you know. This is the real thing and you are making me nervous by hovering."

The Regent chuckled, and then bowed. "As you wish."

Then with two steps back, the Regent raised his starcatcher and brought it down hard.

"Protect," he called in a bold voice to the Royal Draugs.

Immediately, the starcatcher hummed and turned bright gold. He then swiftly pointed his starcatcher to Flora's. The Royal Draugs flew in tiny gold particles to Flora's starcatcher, lighting it up in a glittery haze.

Flora held up her starcatcher, looked at it and then took a deep calming breath. "Protect," she whispered as she cast out the wisp of line, focusing and sending all her energy with the flight.

She guided it straight towards the first star that had arrested her attention. It was the biggest, brightest creation and she knew that was the one. The line reached and strained to make the journey. With a final flick of Flora's wrist, a net opened capturing the large ball of power within. Straining and muscles quivering, she reeled in her prize. Flora then turned and softly placed it at her father's feet. Proud and standing tall, she faced her father and bowed.

"Regent." Her father raised an eyebrow at the formal use of his name.

Flora ignored his reaction. She cleared her throat and continued on. "I am placing at your feet the Legacy of the future Oracle. The star that I have chosen will stay in my keeping until the time of The New Kingdom. The reign where all worlds of enchanting creatures will live in peace and harmony. This I vow." She then relaxed her stance a little bit, peered up to her father and anxiously asked, "Did I say it all right? Do you think Mommy is listening? Because, I could state the vow again." Subconsciously, Flora wrapped her hand around her bell.

The Regent reached down and clasped his daughter's chin,

tilting her head up to meet his gaze. She was the image of her mother Dorothy May, his beloved wife, who once was Oracle of the Pilutars. Now, this young child will take her place. With a heavy sigh, he glanced up to the heavens and prayed silently for his wife's comfort. "You said it perfectly, poppet. Your mother would have been proud to see and hear you speak her chosen words. She has always been a part of you and in your heart. So yes, I believe she is listening and that her spirit will always guide you."

The Regent carefully picked up Flora's chosen star. "Come now, we will bring your treasure inside the Solarium and tomorrow I will write the prophecy that will help guide the future of our world."

With his free hand, the Regent clasped Flora's and together they went through the glass Solarium doors off the catwalk, leaving the starcatchers behind. In anticipation of their entry, a fire came to life within an enormous fireplace.

They walked past the area of the star realms—each star still safe on top of the pillars—and headed straight for the Regent's chambers where he had his personal desk in the far back of the room. On the desk was a glass dome that the Ancient Ones fashioned just for this occasion.

Unbeknownst to them, a dark shadow, hidden in an alcove, watched the two proceed with the coveted star. This presence witnessed the Regent placing the star inside the dome, sealing it within. The shadow's gaze focused entirely on the star where the reflection from the flames in the fire swirled and danced in glory.

"There, poppet," the Regent began as he covered the star with the glass lid.

"Poppet? More like my puppet," the hidden shadow grumbled out of earshot. "I have trained you, Flora, for this moment specifically to catch that star that you think is a legacy, but I will make it MINE! I have lived and breathed in this—this place to the point where I am suffocating. I should have been the Regent! Pathetic code—just because I could not work that contraption call a starcatcher! Therefore, if I can't rule then I will destroy them all, each one painfully slow!"

"Your star will be safe here, Flora," the Regent continued, not hearing or feeling the evil presence. "The Ancient Ones will be very pleased when they hear of your success. I am very proud of you, poppet."

"I did do good, didn't I? I just knew which star was mine, you know. And did you see how I flicked my wrist right? Did you see that I picked the biggest star and I bet you thought it would be too heavy for me." Briefly, Flora stopped her speech and rubbed her sore shoulder, which caused the Regent to slightly smile at her actions. Then the net opened. "I did it, I brought it in just like you!"

"That is right, just like me." The Regent chuckled and skimmed his hand over the top of his daughter's head. "It is time to rest, Flora. You have had a very busy night and tomorrow is a new day with new responsibilities in your training. Come now, I will tuck you in."

The shadow watched them depart before exiting his hiding place. A foot stepped out, followed by flowing black robe. Slowly, the shadow entered into the firelight, and his black robe revealed a Celtic cross. Then a face, filled with hatred, finally emerged. It was Rasoz the sixth Ancient One!

"Simple fools! *Your star will be safe here, Flora.*" Rasoz mimicked with a sneer as he approached the dome. "Nothing is ever safe. One should not presume so. *That* is when mistakes happen. And you, our ever so stately Regent, have made a mistake. You will never feel my hatred because of your so-called love and trust have blinded you to that of reality. Your love for me . . . *your brother.*"

Rasoz quietly lifted the dome exposing the star. As he reached his hand out, a long talon fingernail grew in ugly proportions and with a precise movement, he dug his nail deep inside the star.

Sparks flew and lights flashed! A sharp wind swirled around the Solarium blowing out the fire and threatening the safety of all the pillars housing the realms. An evil laugh exploded from Rasoz as he felt the power contained inside the star. His robe whipped about as the wind twisted around him like a tornado.

"Yes, I can feel it, so much force! Simple-minded fools. They have done everything that I had meticulously planned." He pulled his fingernail out with a scoop motion and completed what he set out to do. There, inside the curve of his nail, was a portion from deep inside Flora's star.

He hid the fragment inside the confinement of his robe and held his hand out and watched as his nail returned to normal.

Wind kept blowing until Rasoz covered the star with the dome. Immediately, the air grew still in an eerie quiet.

"Did I say, nothing is ever safe? Let me retract that and say the power of this piece of star will be safe with me!" With a smug smile, Rasoz left the Solarium, knowing that no one will ever discover the truth of his secret.

CHAPTER 2

The Prophecy

At the first sign of the morning light, the Regent sat at his desk calling upon the Ancient Ones to witness his writing of the prophecy. The writing on this paper will seal the holder's fate when opened and read. There was a plain parchment paper rolled out in front of him, and all six men summoned stood in a single file before him. Belatedly, the Regent realized that his daughter, Flora, should be present too. Within seconds of his summons, a white door with a gold knob appeared in the center of the room.

A red taffeta dress and black high-buttoned boots emerged when the door opened. It was followed by sounds of laughter, whistles and music. As Flora stepped into the Solarium, her clothing turned back into her traditional tulip petal dress that brushed the floor and her hair free flowing with a floral wreath crowning her head.

Flora turned and waved—calling out to her friends. "Bye, bye! Thanks for the rodeo show. I will be back later!" She faced the men in the room and continued her entrance, "Hi everyone! That was great. I just love the Old West playroom.

I have made some great friends there." Then the door to her playroom closed and silently disappeared waiting to be used again at another time.

Briefly, Flora stopped by Rasoz on her way to her father's desk. "Thanks again, Uncle Rasoz for gifting me the doors to play in. Great present! You are the best, you know!"

"Oh, you are welcome, puppet," Rasoz said sarcastically.

"You are so funny, Uncle Rasoz. I keep telling you it is "poppet" not "puppet." Maybe you should just call me Flora from now on."

"Flora, stop teasing Rasoz and approach the desk." The Regent spoke in a firm voice. "Now is the time to be serious; choose a quill to write the prophecy."

Once Flora handed him her choice, the Regent sent gold dust to the pen making it shimmer as he brought it to the paper.

"Why did you do that, Daddy? Oh, I mean, Father," Flora asked.

"My words that are written need to be filled with truth and honor. This prophecy will seal the future along with your star. The Royal Draugs will help me accomplish this. Look closely, Flora—into the glow and tell me what you see," responded the Regent.

Concentrating, Flora reached out and ran a finger through the dust. She watched it travel down her finger to the palm of her hand. She brought her hand closer to her face and focused her eyes on the tiny particles. Gradually, several forms took shape. There were tiny creatures standing on her palm! Each had a bulldog face with battle armor covering their bodies. Large wings spanned out from their backs and within their hands was a shield of honor.

"Those are the Royal Draugs, poppet. They are going to protect the truth of the prophecy."

"Protect," Flora said as she blew the Royal Draug's from her hand to the pen. The gold mist shot out and swirled around the pen making it glow even brighter.

The Regent brought the golden quill to the paper and wrote, reading out loud to the room. "I, Regent, am in the presence of my daughter, Flora, who is pure of heart. She shall be Oracle to the Pilutar Realm. It is her destiny and her successor's that shall be contained within these words I write."

The parchment took on a soft glow with each stroke of the pen. Sparks shot out and flew about the room.

"Father, the pen is making sparks fly off the paper, why is that?"

The Regent stopped his writing and glanced at Flora. "That is the truth being written, poppet." He turned back to his task, "I am in the presence of my six pure-of-heart Ancient Ones."

The sparks stopped!

"Father," Flora whispered, "the sparks stopped. Did you not write the truth?"

A wave of fear hit the Regent.

"Father?" Flora tugged on the sleeve of his robe.

The Regent realized something was not right, and immediately ordered the Ancient Ones out of the Solarium.

"Father, you did not answer me."

"Flora, go and sit by the fireplace. I will call you when I am ready to begin again."

Flora rolled her eyes and headed for the fireplace, mumbling, "Fine, don't answer me. Maybe I should just ask myself the question. Myself would have no choice but to listen and to answer me, you know!"

The Regent ignored Flora's babbling and turned his attention back to the parchment. "What is this?" he asked the Royal Draugs.

A single Royal Draug appeared from the quill standing on

a word the Regent had written. With a single step back, the golden body showed that the word he stood on was "six."

"Show yourself!" The Regent commanded.

The Draug spun in a circle flying off the parchment. The golden haze took on a larger form to where finally a full-sized Royal Draug appeared in front of the Regent's desk. With a formal bow, the Draug addressed him.

"Sire, your truth has been protected as requested."

Completely confused, the Regent looked at his Draug then back to the parchment. With slow movements, he crossed out the word six and wrote five in its place.

Sparks flew from the paper!

"How, how can this be? I have not seen or felt anything amiss. Who? Who is it? Tell me the name!"

"We cannot, sire. There is evil cloaked by goodness. Have caution!" With that said, the Royal Draug went back to true form and joined the rest of the warriors around the quill.

The Regent felt weary, but he continued writing with the truth boldly showing the way. "There will be a new power of great purpose, the Key to the Legacy. An Oracle shall be born that will bear the weight of this responsibility. She will oversee the final battle of the Realms and achieve the peace needed."

He rubbed his face and glanced back at Flora, asleep by the hearth. She is so little that all he could think of was how he could protect her from what the future held.

Sweeping his hand near the quill, he scooped some of the Royal Draugs and blew them towards Flora, ordering them to protect her. The Draugs flew to the sleeping child and entered the tiny bell around her neck, making it glow bright. Reluctantly, he then woke Flora and called her to his side.

Flora rubbed her eyes and smiled. "Sorry, Daddy—um, Father—I fell asleep." Yawning, she went to stand near the desk.

"No worries, poppet. We are going to play a game! But, first I need you to seal the prophecy with a wish. Make it real and pure, child."

"I wish—I wish," Flora chanted with her eyes squeezed tightly shut. Her face broke into smiles and she silently made the thought complete as she laid her hand on the parchment—sealing it.

"Excellent! Now, for the game. Stand back, for you will need the room. This is very, very important. Your star and prophecy need to be hidden until the time of the Keepers." The Regent came around to Flora and clasped her face in his hands. "Once these items are hidden you will forget their place. It will be an elusive memory to be remembered in the distant future. Do you understand, Flora?"

Flora searched her father's face and looked deep into his eyes. She felt some of his fear and that was something she could not understand but she did trust him so with that came the knowledge and wisdom of what was at stake. "I understand. I will hide these for you and for our people."

The Regent sent the prophecy and star to Flora, where it hovered in front of her face. He then stepped away and turned his back, giving her the privacy she needed.

The two were unaware that someone was witnessing everything they were doing. Hidden in the alcove, yet again, stood Rasoz who had seen all. He watched Flora whose back was to him. She lowered her head as if to pray with the star and the prophecy near. So, close! The Regent's back is turned. Is it possible to take them all now? With a tentative step forward, Rasoz exited his hiding place only to jump back when suddenly Flora's arms swept up and out. A brilliantly blinding light caused him to shield his eyes in a reflex, blocking his vision.

The light disappeared and Flora's soft voice spoke in the room, "It is done, Father."

CHAPTER 3

The Veil of Sanctuary

Twenty Years Later

The Pilutars were gifted with a strong affinity with the Natural Earth. With that, they could manipulate earth's structures by using and working with the trees, mountains and land. They had the freedom to walk among the mortals of LaHiere Village. Below Bellmaur Peak, a mountain just outside of the village, children of LaHiere would come to play and their laughter would fill the sky. There were fun-filled pranks and jokes. Natural Earth absorbed the joyful faith of the villagers and in turn gave it to the Pilutars—feeding the gift given to them.

Flora, now Oracle of the Pilutars, watched over the mortals of the village until she made a horrific discovery. A discovery that changed everyone's life whether magical or mortal.

Everyone was living a lie. A lie that Flora must keep a secret. She had known that this time would come—just not in this way. The village will just exist. They will carry on, ignorant to what is happening to them. The changes will be gradual, not sudden. No one will suspect that evil will slowly take over. Would she change anything—knowing what she does now?

She shook her head. She knew that the time spent in LaHiere was something that she would never change.

Like a picture laid out before her, she saw the future and what she must do until the time of the new Oracle.

The one who should be stronger.

The one who could save them all.

With a saddened heart, Flora looked towards her beloved village. They, the mortals, must forget about the Pilutars and all other magical creatures for now. The townspeople will be kept contained within the tiny village; unknowing.

Flora stood at the base of Bellmaur Peak and looked into the meadow where her sacred tulips, the designated symbol of the Pilutars, circled the area in an abundant display. Her lovely, long blonde hair waved around her. Beautiful wild-flowers circled her head with adult antennae standing straight proudly. Ice-blue eyes sparkled on a beautiful porcelain skin face. Brightly colored scarves, shaped like flower petals sewn together by special magic, draped her body. Around her neck hung a bell identical to all the bells around each of her subject's necks, except hers glowed bright as only an Oracle's could.

She raised the bell high into the air and rang it. The twinkling music reached up and threaded throughout the forest. Answering bells could be heard and soon all the Pilutars in her care stood before her in the meadow.

The Ancient Ones, stood in a single row in the front. All five stood proud in their colorful monk-like robes. A bold Celtic-like cross on each of their chests marked the authority gifted to them. She so cherished each of these elders and regrettably was reminded of the empty spot that used to be for the sixth, Rasoz, her uncle who was once she thought a cherished friend. She had discovered Rasoz's life choice was one of greed. Therefore, she was forced along with the help of the other Ancient Ones, to send Rasoz through the Banishing Door, stripping him of his bell and emblem. A mistake that will haunt her for generations.

The Pilutars all stood patiently waiting to hear their Oracle speak. The males all wore similar monk robes and on their heads a skull cap in the bold color of their clan. The women wore a scarf dress and hair braided out of respect to Flora. The large pointed elf-like ears and antennae portrayed their entrance in Full Cycle. Children gathered by their parents' side, their downy fur bodies and elf-like faces full of mischief. These adorable creatures were only in the Seed Cycle and have not yet grown their antennae.

Commanding silence, Flora reached up and clasped her hand around her bell necklace. Matching movements were made throughout the congregation as they, too, held their bells.

Flora's strong voice reached their listening hearts. She told them of the need to create a safe haven to wait out time. A place where their magic will be kept secured.

No questions were asked and with blind faith the Pilutar people twilled a musical sound of agreement, raising their bells into the air. The song from all the bells joined and swirled in a gold protective mist above their united heads, slowly shifting away in a golden path straight into the Natural Earth's ground. The earth rumbled and broke apart to form a magical door with a Celtic-like cross displayed on the front.

The Veil of Sanctuary was formed.

As Flora watched each of her subjects walk through the door of their safe haven, she beckoned the Ancient Ones to her side.

"I must ask for your trust," Flora requested from each of the Ancients. She saw the confusion on their faces and Flora knew that they had questions. Questions that she could not answer.

"We must protect our Veil. Together we will ask the Regent to create a special BellKey that will be used for the preservation of our kind. This BellKey will be in the form of three. They will each have special powers and when joined an ultimate power. All the realms must be aware and protect their own."

The Ancient Ones agreed and formed a circle with Flora in the middle. Then with arms raised high, they joined their bells once again to create. The Natural Earth shook from the power they enforced as they called upon the Skylar Realm for assistance. From their joined bells, a sharp bolt of light pierced the sky. In answer to their call, the Regent sent three separate BellKeys flowing down through the light and into Flora's hands. The first BellKey had the power of strength and will; the second contained growth, love and security; the third, the gift of healing. All three BellKeys could be used to communicate with each bearer and other realms.

Each of the BellKeys looked the same as the ones they wore, just a bit larger. The main difference is that each opened like a locket and could be joined together to form a large bell. When rung it could behold a power of great proportions.

"My dearest friends, you must assign three to be the Bell-Keepers. Choose well! For each BellKey has its own individual power and when worn by the pure soul, the power will stay for the good. Granted, these Keys will protect themselves when worn by the un-chosen but be forewarned, that if ever in the hands of evil, the power will switch to its opposite."

"But, Flora why must we choose? You are the Oracle," stressed one Ancient.

"I am choosing to stay behind and live in the mountain. There I can keep watch over our townspeople. You five must continue in my place. If I should ever need you I will ring my bell for you."

"By going into the mountain and not into the Veil . . . you will slowly lose your gifts. Are you sure this is the choice that must be made?"

"The Draugs will preserve what is needed of mine for the future. This is what was meant to be. The prophecy must prevail. Remember to send word to the other realms."

Reluctantly, the Ancient Ones went through the door to the Veil of Sanctuary using the BellKeys to lock them in. Once the door closed behind them, it slowly faded from sight.

Sighing, Flora knew she needed to see her father one last time. The bell around her neck glowed and sent a small ball of light skimming into the air. Gradually, the light became a white door with a gold knob. Flora briefly remembered receiving the gift of making doors from Rasoz. She could escape for hours at a time playing inside her "playrooms" instead of studying with the Ancient Ones. This time her gift was used to pass through to her father's castle.

Upon her entrance, Flora found herself in the Solarium where her father's huddled form lay still on the stone ground.

"Father!" she cried as she raced forward only to realize that she was blocked.

Golden bars of Royal Draugs surrounded the Regent, completely containing him and the stars in a cage. She glanced around and noted that the four pillars were still intact with the cherished stars and the fifth pillar, the largest of all, still was empty.

A groan came from the Regent as he lifted his head.

"Father! Father! What have you done?" Asked the horrified Flora as she watched the Regent's antennae slowly dissolved away.

"Ah, Flora. I gave you all my strength and power. They are now contained within the BellKeys."

"What? You couldn't! Not now, not when I need you the most!"

"Flora, you have the knowledge. You know what you must do."

Flora's hands wrapped around the gold bars. A feeling of warmth spread up her arms. "And these bars? Are they necessary?"

"Our stars are special, Flora. No one must reach them. All it would take is for someone to destroy a star and then our people will vanish. The Draugs will watch over them and keep them safe. Now, you must carry on as you planned; go and live in Bellmaur Peak. There will be a time when you must fulfill your destiny so that your legacy can live on. I wish you well, poppet."

"But, Father—"

"No, child, you must let me go. You know the path that must be taken. Send me to your LaHiere Village where you can watch over me and learn. There I will keep our people's memory alive with stories. The villagers must not learn of what has transpired but they also must not completely forget about you because the day will come when the new Oracle will be revealed and she must have the townspeople's faith in order to fulfill the legacy."

Flora obeyed his wish and focused on a point behind the Regent. With that single glance, the white door appeared and opened. Through the opening, Flora could see the villagers as they went about their day's work. The Regent stood and stepped through the door. He gave a final glance at his daughter.

"Remember the BellKeys and what they stand for. They are the key to the prophecy."

Flora watched her door fade from sight. Gazing through the golden bars she looked at the stars protected within. Slowly, around each star, a bubble formed. The word had spread! Each realm heard her words of wisdom and are now cocooned—safe and secure from the outside forces.

Flora released herself from the Regent's Solarium and was once again at the base of Bellmaur Peak. On top of the mountain, she found the cave that she likes. She sealed herself inside with the golden dust of Royal Draugs in order to save her magic for as long as possible.

She filled her days watching the village and forest, where her father now lived.

CHAPTER 4

The Blue Mist

Present Day, Two Hundred Years Later

An earthquake hit the Natural Earth with no warning.
Again and again the tremors rattled the LaHiere forest.
There was panic and confusion, and forest animals were racing
to find shelter and seeking safety. But unknown to them, a
new danger was present.

In a grassy field at the far corner of the forest, the scenery
shifted with each quake. The forbidden broke through and a
brown door with a Celtic-like cross appeared with a black
knob. Slowly, it creaked open and a blue foggy mist seeped
out. Slithering, it wound itself rapidly around the field, killing everything in its path, before turning towards the forest.
An evil laugh echoed as the blue haze spread its destruction.

A large buck and his young stopped eating some nearby
grass when they heard the evil laugh. Sniffing the air, the buck
sensed danger but could not find the source. Anyway, the two
thought it best to flee. Right away.

"Hurry, son—we must leave—run for the meadow. Run swift, son."

The two ran for safety but when the father looked back to
encourage his son to run faster, he realized he was too late.

The blue fog had already reached his son who was lying on the ground, still and barely breathing, with a mist wrapped around his body. The buck watched in horror as the haze went in through his son's nose.

"No! No!" he screamed. His hooves pounded as he raced back.

At the sound of his voice, the fog released the baby buck and went farther into the trees, searching for more life to destroy.

Gently, the buck bent his head and cradled his young within his antlers and carried him away.

The townspeople of LaHiere Village worked diligently to repair any damage caused by the earthquake. Some saw that the trees were dying, while others ignored what they could not explain. Madeline D'May Hemis, known as Maddie to the village, was the one person whose heart was being torn in two. She was the one who could not ignore what was happening to the forest.

Standing alone, just before the bridge that led to her cherished area, Maddie watched with tears rolling down her face as all living things wilted and the color sucked away from the woodland area. She was completely helpless and she struggled to understand what she was seeing.

Her parents worked with the others picking up and clearing away the rubble, but Dylan, Maddie's brother, stood silently off to the side watching his sister.

"Mom," Dylan called over to where his parents were working, "I am going to go and check on Maddie."

"No, Dylan. Your father and I need you here." Putting a hand on her back, Mrs. Hemis stretched. Then she wiped her brow and accepted a glass of water from her husband. "This work is not going to get done on its own," she told her Dylan. "And as soon as we are through we are going home to prepare for your sister's 10th birthday party."

"Do you really think a birthday party is a good idea? Look at the forest. It is completely destroyed! Maddie is not going to handle that well and a *party*?"

"Dylan, your mother knows what is best. The birthday party will stand. It will help to get everyone's mind off of this morning," Mr. Hemis said.

"I know, Dad. But this is Maddie we are talking about."

"There are times when you need to let Maddie deal with things on her own, as well as the townspeople," he mumbled under his breath. "We all know that she loves the forest. Sooner or later we will have to look into it. But, our town is part of a disaster area now." Mr. Hemis did not want his son to know but he, too, was very concerned about his Madeline. She is the first female born to his side of the family in more than two centuries. Maddie was a phenomenon that occurred against all odds, therefore all the townspeople treated her like a special treasure and were overprotective to the point of spoiling.

"Come on, Dylan. We are through for now. We need to get home and set up the birthday party. Maddie has a new dress to wear that I know will cheer her up," said Mrs. Hemis with a smile.

As he followed his parents, Dylan mumbled to himself, "Maddie *happy* about wearing a dress? I don't think so."

Another aftershock tremor hit the LaHiere Village area causing treasured cookware to fall, shattering to tiny pieces. Golden walls, filled with elite Royal Draugs, shifted and shuddered as the Natural Earth roared its displeasure, yet again. Scrambling, Flora tried to hide her ample figure under her kitchen table getting stuck between the table legs.

"I knew clothes and chairs could shrink without any warning, I guess tables can too," she pondered out loud. With a fast wiggle of the hips, she made it through. She crouched and waited for the Natural Earth's ride to be complete only to realize that this has been happening too often lately. Abruptly what had started stopped. An eerie silence caused Flora's heart to race.

She blew her bangs out of her face and attempted to leave her hiding place, but got stuck once again.

"Well, this really is pathetic! If I did not know better I would think that one of my Pilutars was shrinking my table!"

Pausing, she asked herself, yet again, out loud, "Do I know better? Ah, you do? You do. I do. I do know better!"

The golden walls of Flora's cave flashed their response.

With a scowl of frustration, Flora glanced at the walls. "Well, I do. I think?" She focused back at the task at hand and placed her hands around the table legs pushing and prodding until she popped out. Standing, she brushed her now gray hair braid away from her face and surveyed the damage to her home. Not too bad. Could be worse! Picking up a cookie sheet, she looked into it and proceeded to have a conversation with herself as one tends to do when one has been devoid of company for 200 years.

"So, what do you think is bringing all the ruckus about?" Flora asked.

The distorted vision showing the once-before young and vital Oracle replied, "That disturbance was very unsettling! You would think that the Skylar Realm would have contacted you to let you know the status of these earthquakes. They are the ones who can manipulate Natural Earth's forces, you know. I believe that it should be looked into immediately."

"Oh, I so agree with you! Why, I was just thinking that myself! It even interfered with my cooking."

"What is that smell?" Sniffing, the young Oracle from within the cookie sheet asked. "Are those your cookies?"

"Cookies! Oh goodness!" Flora raced to her stove and pulled out the bell-shaped cookies that smelled heavenly. She grabbed one off the sheet, waved it in the air to cool off and promptly bit into it.

"Perfect! These are absolutely perfect." With a sigh of relief, Flora leaned into the golden wall of her home. As her back touched the wall a stabbing pain hit her. The cookies fell to the floor as Flora clutched her heart and doubled over.

She looked at the wall and asked, "You are showing me so much pain and sadness, why?"

"Seek and you will know," was the response from the Royal Draugs.

With a deep breath, Flora stretched her hand out, bracing herself for the feelings she knew would come. Palm met the golden stone and what should have been warm was so cold to the touch. Shudders racked Flora's body making her antennae jerk. The Natural Earth's life-force was so very weak.

Flora slowly picked her way through the broken cookware to the golden veil entrance of her home. She grasped her bell and waved her arm, and the veil opened like a curtain gaining the sight to see outside but no one could see within.

Immediately her gaze went to the LaHiere Village. People were repairing the wooden bridge that connected their land to that of the forest. Rushing river water threatened the townspeople, but Flora knew that they would be safe for now. The buildings and homes were intact. She could see the children standing in the streets. No one appeared hurt. It was the sight of the forest that caused her to gasp. What was once full of life now lay dead. No colors; no life. Just a barren existence. The only sound that penetrated the forest air was a black crow cawing while he circled the area. He had a smug look of freedom as his wings spanned out in wild glory.

"By the Tulips, how is this possible? The townspeople would never have done this! No, they never would. This must be researched and whoever or whatever has done this must be stopped."

With her head bowed and hand wrapped around her bell, Flora called upon all her power to the Ancient Ones. Light flashed and the shadow of Flora's full figure could be seen on the golden walls within her home. The bell's music flowed and Flora called upon the ones that she had help create. The ones she had hoped they would never need.

The BellKeepers . . .

CHAPTER 5

The BellKeepers

The hovering interlocked BellKey entered the forest guiding the final entrance of the three BellKeepers. With a unison clap of the three Pilutars, the BellKey disengaged and became three separate BellKeys. Their hands reached out and claimed their treasure promptly securing it around each of their necks. The door to the Veil of Sanctuary faded to a pinprick of light that silently disappeared.

With a single step on the deaden forest ground, grass sprouted. More grass grew as they walked making a green pathway, the only color visible.

Modie led the way, skipping with the energy that only a 10-year-old can achieve. With each skip-fall footprints of green were created in a zigzag pattern. As he turned around to see what he made, he laughed and skipped backgrounds to complete his tracks making a solid green path.

His parents, Jamar and Ashlar, walked a bit slower taking in the reality of the task ahead of them.

The red color of Jamar's skullcap gleamed as a ray of sunlight pierced through the forest trees offering its approval of the task ahead. His monk-like robe swayed as he walked forward. His chiseled cheekbones and a stubborn chin gave him the appearance of a strong-willed man. Elf-like pointed ears and antennae betrayed his ancestry, a fact that he wore proudly.

After he circled the area—examining and surveying the immediate damage—Jamar picked up a blade of grass and sniffed it. His touch then skimmed a nearby tree before he concluded as fact—"Fire did not do this! There is no evidence of burning cinders. Yet, the area has the look of an inferno. It is still and quiet and lifeless. I don't believe that the Ancient Ones realize the depth of destruction that awaited us here."

Holding his BellKey in his hand, Jamar breathed in deep and closed his eyes. He tried to find the source of the problem. Power shimmered through his body as the BellKey grew warm to his touch. Strength and will poured from his BellKey, flowing out and grasping each dying creation. Greedily, the immediate area drank but, each time Jamar tried to seek about the cause he failed. The area did not know or was just too afraid to speak the truth. With a sigh he let go of the BellKey and turned to his wife who stood off to the side.

"There are no answers to be found. This section, though, has accepted my gift of strength. But, it still lay frozen. It is your turn, with your BellKey, to give it the love and guidance needed to flourish." His elf-like ears twitched with frustration for not knowing what really happened here. And to protect this forest in the future they somehow need to know.

Ashlar guided her BellKey to her lips and offered a kiss. Her mother's love embraced the life around her. Pine and aspen trees flourished with moss quietly creeping on the trunks. Grass and shrubs filled the woodland. Color invaded the gray like paint by number set. Ashlar, with her porcelain-smooth skin and white braided hair, smiled and glowed with satisfaction as she let go of her BellKey.

"Well, this is a start but the animals and other creatures will need to be called and healed if needed. Modie's exuberance and his unique gift of communicating with them and his Bell-Key's power of healing will take care of that. Now, where did that boy go off to?" Looking around, Ashlar saw Modie a short distance away completely absorbed with doing karate kicks on an imaginary foe.

Modie's round furry body with its young elf face crouched down in anticipation of his enemy's next move.

"Hieeeeya!" With his arms flowing and then pausing in a classic karate stance, Modie challenged, "Come forward and fight, if you dare! I, Modie the Third BellKeeper, will protect all that are worthy!"

"Modie, come here!" called Ashlar.

"You have been spared for now but we shall meet again!" With a final karate kick in the air, offered as a parting shot to his evil enemy, Modie rushed over to where his parents were waiting.

Ashlar looked down at her son who was absently rubbing his hand on her petal skirt, the ends tickling his palm. With her firm voice, she commanded his attention that tended to wander. "Modie, your father and I have finished this area of the forest. We need you to do your job now."

"Okay, Mom. Do you know what happened here?"

"No, son. Your father tried to get a feel of the area but there are no answers. If we still struggle in finding the reason we will contact the Ancient Ones for guidance."

"So, while I am working can I explore too? Maybe I can find something."

Ashlar looked at Jamar, who nodded.

"You can explore while you work, Modie. But only where there is color! We will continue to the left towards the mountain. You can start on the right where the color begins. Keep a close eye out for any animals that may need your help. Just remember to stay within the color. It will be safe there."

Immediately, Modie headed out to explore.

"We will ring your BellKey to let you know when you should head back towards the mountain," Ashlar called out as Modie scrambled away.

CHAPTER SIX

Mighty Modie

I can't believe I have to wear this stupid dress!"

Maddie Hemis, who turned 10 years old today, stomped her way across the wooden bridge that led to the LaHiere Forest. Lilac-colored taffeta adorned with delicate ribbons made a crinkling sound of protest from her actions. Her lucky ball cap, stuffed with hair, sat defiantly on her head as a show of rebellion much to her mother's dismay.

"Stupid party! No one MY age came! Just adults. Nobody likes to play with me. I don't know why they came anyway."

In a sing-song voice she mimicked her parents. *"Sit up straight. Maddie stop climbing those trees. Maddie why, can't you be a little lady? Maddie, you will wear this new dress for your birthday party!"*

"Well, I showed them! I am going to go and play even if it is by myself! No frilly parties for me! Just because it is my birthday does not mean that I want a party. Just because I said that I would *wear* the dress, well, that did not mean that anyone could *see* me in it!"

Once she crossed the bridge, Maddie ran up the hill that led to the meadow. Here she felt a deep sense of belonging and considered this place her very own. A place where she can be herself, not like in the village where everyone, especially her family, thought she should act like a lady.

With a heavy sigh, she realized that nothing had changed. The meadow and forest still looked empty. She wanted the grass to grow again so that she can try to find a four-leaf clover. She wanted the trees to have strong branches so that she could climb up and pretend that she was the Queen of the Forest overseeing all her royal subjects below. What Maddie really wished for was a miracle.

Bending down, Maddie picked up a dead dandelion. She scrunched her eyes tightly closed and made a wish—blowing the white weed petals into the wind. A soft breeze whisked them into the forest as Maddie continued to whisper, "I wish—I wish—I wish," in a silent chant.

As if in answer to her plea, a beautiful butterfly flew from the forest, its delicate wings whispering through the dead flower's petals. Maddie was quite amazed and watched the flight.

"Where did *you* come from? I did not think those flower wishes really worked."

The butterfly hovered in front of Maddie's face. Giggling, she reached up to catch it but the butterfly fluttered back.

"Where are you going?"

In response, the butterfly flew off back towards the forest. Maddie chased it, calling out in dismay, "Wait, wait for me!"

Holding her ball cap on with one hand, Maddie raced into the forest only to come to a skidding halt.

With her mouth wide open, Maddie watched the color race across the forest. The butterfly whisked back to Maddie, who was batting it away with her hand. She could not believe that her wish was coming true right before her eyes! In rapid movements the butterfly brought Maddie's attention back to it.

"What? What is it?" she asked. "Do you want me to follow you?"

Again, the butterfly took off racing with the color in a zigzag motion. Maddie scrambled and struggled to keep up.

"Slow down! You are going too fast," she huffed. Her breath was coming out in sharp spurts with a pain starting in her side. Maddie half walked, half ran, deeper into the forest.

Hearing a gurgle of water ahead, she burst through a clump of trees. A smile flashed on her face when she saw the stream where Dylan and Jake taught her how to skip stones.

Gingerly, she made her way down the slope to the trickling stream. She sat down on a nearby rock and pulled her shiny white patent leather shoes off and then stuffed the too frilly socks inside them. Wiggling her toes with freedom, Maddie plunged her feet into the cool water with a splash.

Modie held his BellKey in his left hand as he trudged through the now living area of forest. As his imagination took flight, he pretended the forest was his kingdom. There was a disaster and some of his subjects may be injured. It was up to him to find and protect all that needed him, Modie the Third Bell-Keeper. Through his thoughts he wished for playmates. He grabbed a hold of his BellKey and pretended to call his "men."

"Stand by! I have explored the north and found it clear. I am heading west to the edge of our land. Wait, I am being ambushed!" He heard sounds and rustling, animals escaping their hiding places. A squirrel scrambling on top of a tree dropped a prized acorn on Modie's head causing him to rub the sting away. "False alarm, men! Over and out!"

Suddenly, Modie heard some movement behind some newly awakened brush and he transferred his attention to the sound. Bending down in a crouch, he peered beneath the bush and saw a large, trophy antler buck bedded down next to a smaller deer. Upon sensing Modie's presence, the buck scrambled up and lowered his head, antlers jutted forward. With a snort and stomp, the buck warned Modie.

"Back away! You are not welcome here!"

Forewarned in his mind, Modie used his unique ability and sent word to the magnificent animal. *"It is okay, I promise. I am a BellKeeper, here to help the forest. Is he sick?"* Modie motioned to the fallen deer as he continued forward with caution.

"This is my son."

The buck sensed that Modie really was not a threat, so he relaxed. With his black nose, he nudged his offspring and received no response. *"The blue mist came and he could not escape. I watched it go into his body. I just could not get him away fast enough. I think—I think he is dying."*

"Let me come and see him," Modie said.

The buck took a single step back but still stayed close with a watchful eye. *"He is all I have left."*

Modie crawled over to the deer, keeping himself on the same level as the fallen animal. With his eyes tightly closed, Modie started at the hindquarters. He ran his hands over the animal's body, whose chest was rising and falling but in an uneven rhythm. There was a poison inside that Modie sensed was destroying the baby deer!

Modie continued with his task guiding his hands and searching. When he reached its head, he felt two small knobs, which surprised him. He opened his eyes and said in awe, "You have antennae!" Sure enough, this fallen animal had two small black knobs on the top of his head, portraying him as a young button buck. "One day I will have antennae, too!" said Modie.

"*Will Button Buck live?*" the father asked anxiously.

Ignoring the father's question, Modie took his BellKey and laid it on the button buck's chest.

A golden glow surrounded Modie and the young animal. Scrunching his eyes closed, Modie willed the poison into the BellKey. Slowly, the baby buck breathed easier and opened his eyes.

"*Dad?*" muttered the young buck.

"*I am here, my Button Buck. All is well.*" The father looked at Modie who was now standing, grinning from ear to ear. "*Thank you, thank you so much. I owe you a debt of gratitude.*"

With a sheepish look, the baby deer, quite grateful, said to Modie, "*Thank you.*"

"*You saved Button Buck! You have mighty powers, a truly mighty creature,*" acknowledged the father.

"*Ah, it was nothing,*" Modie said as he kicked a small stone. "*Just doing what I was sent here to do-ahh-umm-Sir-and umm-Button Buck.*"

In a shy, quiet voice Button Buck whispered, "*You can call me B.B.*"

"*And you can call me Modie!*"

"*If you should ever need my help, Mighty Modie, I will be there for you,*" assured the father as the two reunited pair scrambled off into the sanctuary of the living forest.

Modie felt so much pride as he continued with his exploring.

He saw a little stream ahead—rushed over and looked at his reflection. The signature color of his clan—red, flecked with orange—blinked back at him. He moved his elf-like ears that was attached to his cherub face back and forth giggling at the picture he made. But, no antennae had grown. They won't until he reached the Bud Cycle. Looking around the ground, Modie found two acorns, which he picked and placed on top of his head. He grinned as he looked back at his reflection.

A sudden splash brought Modie's head up. There was something sitting on a rock.

Cautiously, Modie crept over to stand behind the creature. Bending over its shoulder he looked into the water and saw his reflection next to it.

"Hi!" said Modie.

"Aaaaagh!" Shrieking Maddie fell into the stream bottom first. The water sprayed out soaking Modie's furry body and completely drenching Maddie's birthday dress.

Modie reached out and grabbed the ball cap off Maddie's head. Her long blonde curls came spilling out. Icy blue eyes blinked water away as she gazed up at Modie.

"Ohhhh, you look like a little Oracle!" Modie said in awe dropping the cap.

"No, silly! My name is Maddie. I am from LaHiere Village. Where are you from?" With a frown forming on her face, she said, "You look different from me but that is okay because I am different too. And your eyes! I never met anyone with red eyes before. You even have a furry body like my teddy bear at home. Who are you?"

With a feeling of importance, Modie stood. "I am *the* Mighty Modie. One of the BellKeepers!"

Gasping, Maddie scrambled out of the water and grabbed Modie's hand. "Did you say BellKeeper? Are you sure? You aren't playing a joke? My granddad always told me the story about the Pilutars and the Legend of the BellKeepers, but he said they were just fairy tales. I knew it was for real. I just knew it! I can't wait to tell Dylan. I told him it was real. But, no! He didn't believe it. And here you are! A Pilutar in MY forest."

Embarrassed now, Modie glanced down and started kicking rocks into the stream. "Well, yes, I'm a Pilutar and a BellKeeper. It is really nothing though."

"Hey, do you know what happened to my forest?" Maddie's blue eyes implored Modie.

"My parents and I have been sent here to find out, but we don't have any answers yet." Coming out of his daze, Modie realized that this is someone he could play with. "I have work to do but you can come with me and help me explore the forest but only where there is color. That is where it is safe."

"Oh, I love to explore! And the forest is the best place to find things. Before everything died, I would come here almost everyday."

"Great, come on then," said Modie as he bent down and picked up Maddie's ball cap from the ground.

"I know this forest pretty good so I will help you," offered Maddie as she covered her mouth with both hands then looked at Modie with awe.

"I am *helping* a BellKeeper," said Maddie in disbelief.

She reached for her cap and put it on her head and took hold of Modie's hand as they crossed the stream.

"Since I am helping you does that mean I am your assistant? Or better yet a *BellKeeper* like you? Do I get a BellKey, too? I think I am going to need a BellKey!"

"Maddie, you can't have a BellKey," said Modie, with exaggerated patience.

The animals continued to come out following Modie and Maddie. They stayed a safe distance behind as if to watch over them.

Suddenly, a cawing sound came from an unusually large black crow with a streak of white on its head. It was perched on a nearby tree watching the children carefully. With a fake yawn and a rolling of the eyes, the crow took off in flight over their heads.

Modie and Maddie watched as the bird flew in a circling motion before flying off deeper into the forest.

"I have never seen that bird before. Who has ever heard of a crow with white feathers?" asked Maddie.

"Maybe we should follow it."

"I don't think we should, Modie. My mom says that deep inside the forest is not safe anymore."

With his chest stuck out in pride, Modie responded, "Well, *my mom* says it is safe where there is color. That bird is black, which is a color so, we can follow him. Besides, I am a Bell-Keeper and I can protect you."

He grabbed Maddie's hand, "Hurry, Maddie, before he gets away!"

Modie followed the black crow to the end of the colored forest but Maddie started to hang back. The animals that had been following them refused to go farther, too.

"I don't think this is a good idea, Modie." Maddie said nervously as she glanced around. "It is creepy here. Really, really creepy."

"*It isn't safe, Modie! Danger, beware.*" The animal warnings whispered through Modie's mind.

Gazing out from the colored edge, Modie watched the crow land on top of an old door sitting in the middle of the dead field. Completely dimensional, the door could be seen from all angles. Nothing appeared to be holding it up. The door, dirty brown in color, sagged with age and a familiar Celtic-like cross was on the front.

"Maddie, you stay here. I am going to take a closer look at that door."

"Wait, Modie! You can't go over there," cried Maddie.

The animals begged him too, but Modie would not listen.

"Everything will be fine," reassured Modie and continued his approach. "It looks like a Pilutar door. Except it is really old." He paused and ran his fingers across it. "Probably hundreds of years."

"Why don't you open it and see what is inside."

"Huh?" Modie looked up at the crow.

"Go on, explore inside. You will find some amazing things."

Modie reached for the black knob and turned it. With a creak the door opened and a blue mist seeped out. The crow left his perch and flew near the mist flapping its feathers, pushing the vapor towards Modie.

The mist slithered to Modie's feet, winding up his legs. He looked down and watched the motion in a trance-like stare. Slowly it crept up his body wrapping itself around him like a vine. Round and round, the mist became a rope pulling Modie towards the door. The shape of a hand appeared from the foggy vine and began tugging on the BellKey around Modie's neck. Modie could barely hear Maddie's voice.

"Modie! Modie!"

"Can't move, I can't breathe," Modie thought to himself. His arms hung limp by his side in defeat.

"MODIE! You can't breathe?" How Maddie knew this, she did not know, but she could feel it. "Hang on, Modie!"

Racing towards Modie, her tiny legs pumping as fast as possible, Maddie let loose a horrific scream as she slammed her slight body into Modie's causing the hold of the mist to break loose and release the BellKey along with her new best friend. Rolling as they hit the ground, their young bodies absorbed the impact.

The crow flew circling once around Modie and Maddie before flying out towards the mountain. His cawing could be heard echoing through the forest but to Modie it sounded like laughter.

Maddie anxiously looked at Modie who was lying still on the ground. She grabbed him around his face in a panic. "Modie! Can you breathe now? Are you all right? I know that PCR or that CP something that can help you breathe. I think I can do it."

"Maddie, I am fine." Sitting up and shaking his head, Modie looked at Maddie with wonder. "I can't believe what just happened! Did you see what that crow did? There was this hand, grabbing me. Thanks, Maddie! You protected me and I am the one that is supposed to protect you. Some BellKeeper I am! But, how did you know? How did you know that I could not breathe?"

"I don't know." Maddie shrugged her shoulders and stood up. "I just did, you know. I heard your voice in my head and I just *knew* you needed my help." Gasping, Maddie covered her mouth with her hands, yet again. "I really helped a Bell-Keeper. I *saved* you! Can I have a BellKey now?"

Sighing, Modie looked at his new friend with a slight smile. "No, Maddie. You can't have a BellKey now."

Maddie reached out her hand and helped Modie stand. "Fine, but one day I will have a BellKey or something." And then in afterthought she continued, "You are right though. I should have to do a lot more to get one of those. I haven't quite earned it yet, you know. But I will, you'll see."

"Maddie, it's not a thing you earn."

Maddie stopped listening to Modie when she saw the door creaked open again. Her stomach turned at the thought of the blue mist coming back out.

Modie looked at his friend and saw that her face was turning white and was shaking. "Hey, Maddie! Are you okay?"

Stammering, Maddie answered, "I want to go home now. We need to leave this place."

"No, we can't leave yet. That door needs to be shut! I don't know what that mist is but it can't be good for the forest." Taking a deep breath, Modie charged the door. "Hieeeeya!" With a flying karate kick Modie's foot connected with the door.

Behind the door the scenery shifted. A bold suction sound could be heard. Fascinated, Modie watched as the brown door was sucked into thin air.

"Maddie, did you see?" Stopping, Modie realized that she was gone for Maddie was already running to the safety of her home.

As Modie walked back to the colored area, he silently hoped that his new friend would come back. He still had work to do though and that door with the mist would be something his father would want to hear about.

A ringing music filled his elf-like ears. He looked down and he noticed that his BellKey was calling. It was time for him to meet his parents at the mountain.

He grudgingly started to walk, feeling his heart slowly calm down after the adventure he and Maddie just had.

CHAPTER 7

Zosar and Noir

Sitting on a fallen hollow log, Zosar cradled a dead flower in his massive hands. His head was bowed and shoulders shook with silent laughter. He stood and faced Bellmaur Peak, raising the dead flower in a silent salute to his nemesis. A soft breeze pulled at the brittle offering causing a single petal to float to the ground. Stronger the wind became whipping Zosar's hooded robe out and with unholy glee the laughter that he kept contained exploded. The sound echoed around the lifeless mountain.

"Oh, my dearest Flora. You have failed your cherished townspeople and their forest. Do you even know who I am? Do you know how I have waited for this day? How much I endured because of you and your beliefs?" Zosar ranted, knowing full well that Flora would probably not answer since she locked herself inside her golden home.

"Do you see this dead flower? Do you see—" Pausing, Zosar felt a warmth coming from the flower. The drab brown color of the stem was slowly filling with life. Lush green leaves appeared and brilliant colorful buds formed.

"What is happening?" In shock, Zosar whirled around, his robe flying. The single black orb colored eye that was exposed from his masked face searched for the cause of this treachery. A living and breathing forest greeted his probing gaze.

"No, no this can't be!" he yelled. Facing the mountain again, he raised his fist that held the flower. "You did this, didn't you? How could you of done this? There is no way your power is this great now."

Pacing with disgust, he felt his footsteps touching upon soft dewy grass. The new green growth under his feet made his stomach turn with anger that was fed with each footfall.

Hand in hand, Jamar and Ashlar worked their way through the forest towards Bellmaur Peak enjoying the creations that they brought to life once again. Jamar spied a thriving flower shrub, so he bent down and picked a beautiful white hibiscus and placed it into Ashlar's hair.

With a gentle kiss on his wife's brow he said, "We need to rest some now. Why don't you call Modie and have him meet us here. We are just about at the base of the mountain."

Holding her BellKey with two hands, Ashlar silently called for Modie. "It is a time for rest, I agree, Jamar. But, first we need to establish our home. Our work needs to be monitored and we need to find out what happened to this area. I believe that—do you hear something?"

Listening, Jamar's ears twitched. "Yes, I do. It sounds as if someone is in great pain!"

Jamar and Ashlar ran to the base of the mountain and saw a cloaked figure with arms spread wide, a single flower crushed in its firm grip. The sounds coming from it were heartwrenching.

Hearing footsteps, Zosar stiffened. With a roar he whipped his body around ready to attack the intruders of what he considered HIS domain.

Jamar immediately stood in front of his wife offering his protection. With his hands out as a sign of peace he calmly spoke, "We mean you no harm. We are here to help the forest. We heard your cries and thought you may need our assistance."

Ashlar peered around her husband's shoulder and took in the situation. This person, if you could call it that, was not of the forest. His head was covered by a dark hood that circled around to mask most of his face. Only one eye was exposed that seemed to peer through a person's soul. Black and lifeless. His robe, dirty and frayed with a faded area around the chest, caught Ashlar's attention. It so reminded her of something but she just could not grasp the memory. A feeling of dread prickled up her spine.

She clutched Jamar's shoulder tighter and whispered, "Careful, I am sensing danger."

A million thoughts were going through Zosar's mind as he looked upon the two standing before him. *Pilutars! How quaint, how absolutely perfect! How,* pausing Zosar spied the identical objects around their necks. *By the Tulips! Those can't be the Bell-Keys . . . or could they?*

Zosar immediately relaxed his stance and with a great show of humility bowed his head, bringing his hands before him as if to pray.

"Forgive me, newcomers. I was only startled by your approach. No one has been in the area for some time now. You say you are healers of the forest? So, is it you that has been bringing the life back?" Walking towards the area that had regrown, Zosar waved his hand across the expanse. "You have accomplished a miracle. Why, just now I was screaming at the sky for the pain that had been caused." He glanced up to see if he was believed by these Pilutars, the bane of his existence.

Guiding Ashlar to his side, who did so reluctantly because she did not completely trust this man, Jamar spoke, "My name is Jamar and this is my wife, Ashlar. We are called the Bell-Keepers and—"

"The BellKeepers! My goodness, I have heard of the Legend but did not quite believe it!" Zosar said in feigned shock. "It is a deep honor to meet you!" Extending his hands he clasped both Jamar and Ashlar's hands. "I am called Zosar. My friend and I are the only ones that made it through the disaster. The others ran and hid. Maybe now they will come out and enjoy the *peace* only you can provide," he said, gulping down the disgust.

"Your friend, you say? And who is that?" asked the doubting Ashlar.

"Noir, my crow. I, ahh, found him injured. Yes! He was injured," replied Zosar. "Actually, you can hear him now."

In the distance a cawing sound came forth that drew closer. The black crow swooped down and landed on Zosar's shoulder. Absently, Zosar stroked the bird's gleaming feathers.

"Noir, my pet, these people are the BellKeepers and are here to *help* us with the forest." He then turned his attention back to Jamar and Ashlar and said, "Please let me assist you. I can be a great asset since I know this area well."

Husband and wife looked at each other with some doubt. Should they trust a stranger with their secrets? True, he does know the forest and since they were still foreign to the area his knowledge could help them find the reason for the vast destruction.

Sensing their thoughts and possible weakening, Zosar rushed on. "You are probably leery, for that I understand. But, please look at the facts. I was here when everything happened. Noir and I have scavenged this forest for nourishment, living off of whatever survived."

"And what EXACTLY happened here, Zosar?" Ashlar demanded in a strong motherly voice.

"That, my dearest, I can not answer totally. I do know that it originated at the far end of the forest near a clearing. There was a deep rumbling that caused the ground to shake and vibrate." Acting agitated, Zosar started to pace back and forth. "I remember seeing a mist before I was thrown to the ground hitting my head. That is all I remember because I must have blacked out. When I came to, the forest was just gone. There was a foul smell in the air that seemed to close off my breathing. I remember being very disorientated. My face was severely burned, forcing me to wrap my disfigurement from the stares of the villagers. I was so afraid of scaring the children that I have hidden myself here in the forest and mountain. Noir is the one who guided me to the caverns where we have made our home."

He stood still and faced them imploring his case. "Please, you must let me help. If anything I can show you the inside of the mountain. There are dangerous areas that must be avoided. Even BellKeepers would not be safe if ventured too far." With a sly grin that could not be seen, he watched their faces as they made decisions. *Stupid, Pilutars! They cannot even hide their thoughts. So good and pure they are.*

"You are correct that we would need assistance. Especially with the mountain if it is as dangerous as you say," Jamar started.

"Oh, most definitely!" declared Zosar.

Turning to Ashlar, Jamar reasoned. "We must think of Modie and his curious mind. He could get into all kinds of mischief."

"Modie! Yes, we must ask Zosar for his help!" Her mother's overprotective imagination immediately conjured a million things that Modie could get into. His safety was a major concern for them.

"Forgive me, but who is Modie?" Zosar inquired.

"Why, our son the third BellKeeper," answered Ashlar.

Walking towards Ashlar, Zosar stopped a very short distance away. Too close in Ashlar's opinion, since she still did have some reservations about this man.

Zosar's exposed eye gleamed as he focused on the BellKey around her neck. Protectively, Ashlar wrapped her hand around it.

"Charming little bauble you have there. Do all *three* of you have one?" As he tried to reach out as if to touch it, Ashlar half turned her body away to avoid the contact.

"To answer your question—yes, there are only three. And you must not EVER try to touch any of the BellKeys while around our neck. They would be forced to protect themselves because they would not know that you meant no harm—"

"You are correct, madam. I would never harm the Bellkeys," he paused nodding his head towards the necklace.

"Perfect! Now that we are in agreement, we can continue on with the mission," Jamar said as he stood by Zosar's side. "But, first we must secure our lodging. Zosar, please show us the way." As he patted Zosar on the back, he felt an object hidden in the confines of Zosar's robe.

"What is that?"

Squawking, Noir's wings expanded showing his dislike that his master was touched. Taking a few steps back, Jamar eyed the bird warily.

"Easy Noir, there is no threat here." Reaching over his shoulder, Zosar's hand disappeared into his robe, pulling out a large stick that was whittled to resemble a staff. Perched atop the staff was a brilliant clear stone.

"This stone is a heirloom. It has been in my family for 200 years. Whenever I need Noir I just raise it in the air. The sunlight refracts and causes a flashing signal that he responds to.

Quite simple really and is of no value to you." Calmly, Zosar replaced the stick back into its hiding place. "Now, come. I will show you the caverns."

Zosar stood in the middle of the two BellKeepers. He placed his hands on their backs and started to guide them to an entrance at the base of the mountain.

Meanwhile, coming out of the forest, the first thing Modie saw were his parents with a tall stranger. The second thing was the black bird sitting on the stranger's shoulder.

"That is the bird! What is it doing around my parents?"

Quite determined, Modie charged the group.

"Hieeeeya!" Legs first, Modie karate-kicked the back of Zosar's knees hoping to dislodge the bird from the stranger's body.

A shooting pain went through Zosar's legs as they buckled then righted themselves. Noir cawed his displeasure; Zosar's roar and Ashlar's gasp all echoed together.

Reaching down, Zosar grabbed the scuff of Modie's neck and lifted him like he was a puppy getting ready to be scolded.

"I take it that this is yours?" Zosar said to Modie's parents as he promptly dropped Modie to the ground who landed with a thud.

Modie looked up and faced the disapproval on his parents' faces. Ashlar had her hands on her hips, a single foot tapping in time with her anger. Jamar's mouth was set in a firm line as he waited for the explanation to come.

"Well, Modie? What do you have to say for yourself?" he asked.

Jumping up, Modie proceeded to tell them all that had happened to him. "There was this girl Maddie from the village and that black bird." (Pointing accusingly at Noir.) "This brown door was there where there is no color and a blue mist grabbed my throat and started to choke me." Hands clasping his throat, Modie made several gasping sounds. "That bird is the one that sent the mist to me."

"*Excuse me!* Did you just say *no color?* What did we tell you about staying only in the colored areas?" Ashlar demanded.

"But, Mommy, the bird—"

"No, young man! I do not want to hear about a bird or anything else for that matter. You owe Mr. Zosar an apology along with his friend, Noir the black bird."

"Daaad?" Whining, Modie looked at his father hoping that he would understand and listen. But, Jamar was shaking his head in disappointment.

"You deliberately disobeyed us. Now, apologize!"

"Yes, sir." Facing Zosar, Modie apologized even though he thought it was so unfair.

"Once we have our living quarters established, you will need to stay inside for the rest of the day and think about following our rules," stressed Jamar.

Noir, still sitting on Zosar's shoulder, ruffled his feathers in glee. Zosar had a sickening grin on his masked face as he led Jamar and Ashlar into the mountain.

Modie trudged along following the three and all along he kept thinking, "Why won't anyone believe me?"

CHAPTER 8

The Dead End

Why won't anyone believe me?"

In her living room, Maddie faced down a group of people ranging from her brother's friends to adults who were all sitting in the living room staring at her. As she looked down, she saw her birthday dress dripping water all over the clean carpet and that mud was tracked through the house that her mom worked so hard to clean for the party. Her ball cap was the only item that seemed to survive the ordeal. Some of the adults were looking at her with horror. Others just thought it was another Maddie episode.

"I am telling the truth! The BellKeepers are REAL! I met Modie, he is one. We even battled evil. I think we found something that could be killing the forest! And, oh! Oh, I saved his life! You know, Modie, the one I was just talking about!"

There was no response to her impassioned plea. Whispered comments could be heard but no one would give Maddie the audience she wanted.

Racing to her mother, whose face seemed to be getting

redder by the minute, she begged yet again, "Please, Mom! You have got to believe me! The forest is fixed now because of them. But, there *is* something bad there. I saw it!"

A quiet comment came from behind her.

"You might as well give up, Maddie. You know she is not going to listen." Then she ticked off the reasons with his fingers: "(a) you ruined your new dress; (b) you left your party by sneaking out; and (c) most of all you tracked mud into the house."

Turning, Maddie saw Dylan. Surely, he would believe her. "Dylan! Wait until I—"

"Don't rely on me! You are going to have to dig yourself out of this one all by yourself." With a hand in one pocket of his jeans that had a crease in them (giving them a freshly ironed look), Dylan stood there trying to appear older than his 12 years, with his perfectly blonde-spiked hair and freshly washed white T-shirt. If anyone got too close they would swear that he was wearing his father's after-shave.

Frankly, his baby sister's outburst was semi-embarrassing since Joelle, his best friend Jake's twin sister, was here and heard it all. This was the girl that he had not been able to say one word to all year and that is not because he did not have the opportunity. The girl whose raven black hair and green eyes made his heart stumble. The girl who caused him to get a "D" on the Algebra test because he was daydreaming about her when the lesson was taught.

Dylan glanced over and he could see that she was watching and listening to everything he said, *darn!*

Wiping his sweaty palms on his clean jeans, Dylan bent down and whispered in his sister's ear, "Quiet, Maddie! You can tell me all about it later but right now is not the time."

"Madeline D'May Hemis!"

"Oh no! She used my full name, I am in for it now," Maddie mumbled to herself.

"Just look at you! Coming into my home that I worked so hard to get clean just for you. For your birthday party! And if that is not enough, you ruined your new dress and told stories about why you left as if you could justify that action in the first place."

"But, Mom—"

"Don't you 'but' me! You can go upstairs after you say your apologies for being so rude to your guests. You need to think about your actions!"

Muttering a quick apology, Maddie stomped up the stairs with the thudding sound shaking some pictures on the wall. To add another flair, Maddie slammed her bedroom door closed thinking the whole time that it just was not fair!

Inside the natural cave, it took Modie's eyes a few seconds to adjust to the change of light. Manmade torches lined the interior walls obviously put there by Zosar. Above the high entrance were a few bats hanging by their feet. Their bright red eyes alert to the newcomers.

One bat that saw Modie watching him saluted with respect. *"I am called General Alucard, Alu for short. Welcome!"*

Modie grinned and saluted back his new friend. "Thank you. I am glad to meet you and your troops. My name is Modie. Maybe you and your men can be my soldiers."

"Sounds like smashing fun. We will be standing guard for you."

Spying his parents ahead talking to Zosar who stood before an intersection of two separate tunnels, Modie inched forward, his feet padding on the hard-packed earth and his downy body hugging the wall. He really did not want to be here right now. His feelings were so hurt that his adventure was not believed.

Sensing his thoughts, Noir, still perched on Zosar's shoulder, turned his beady eyes on Modie, his beak turned up in a knowing grin. *"A mighty BellKeeper you are not! They will not believe you, ever. I am too good."*

The crow's thought entered Modie's mind. Sticking his tongue out at the creature in a typical childish way, Modie then kicked the cavern wall. A small tunnel appeared that went through the mountain and exited outside. Fully intending to escape, Modie took a step forward only to be stopped.

"Don't even think of going through that tunnel, Modie! This is not the time to use your Pilutar gifts." His father spoke firmly. "You have to help us here and then there is the matter of you thinking about following rules."

"Seal it Modie and then come here immediately. Zosar is explaining some important details to us and you need to listen to what he says," Ashlar ordered.

With a sigh he joined the group with his head down and shoulders slumped. "This has not been a fun day," he mumbled.

"As I was saying before we were interrupted," Zosar said as he glanced down, with a look of exasperation, at the troublesome child. "There are two tunnels. You must always take the right one. Upon exploring the left [at the word *"exploring"* Modie's ears perked right up as this was his favorite word], I found it was a complete waste of time since it was a dead end."

Modie looked at the tunnel that led to the left and wondered, what is a dead end?

"Dad, what is a dead end?"

"Not now, Modie!" Jamar said as Zosar cleared his throat.

"As I was saying, yet again, please follow me, and I will show you an empty chamber that you could probably make use of."

A short distance down the right tunnel, they encountered a key hole formation along the wall. Crouching through they all entered the exposed cavity. The BellKeeper family surveyed what was to become their new home. A large open space, completely devoid of any remnants from previous tenants, opened before them.

With a smile Ashlar turned to her family and said, "Ready?"

The family of three used their cherished gift from the Regent. The traditional golden glow appeared casting eerie shadows along the walls. The ground shifted and a rock formation emerged from the ground that was flat at the top. Perfect for a table! Other formations followed and served as small stools to sit on. Walls on either side shook and two cavities were made. Generous green ivy grew and covered the areas as curtains for privacy. There they would rest when needed. Shelves and pottery all made from the Natural Earth were stacked for future use. The ceiling roared and a small shaft bore through letting in the beloved sunlight causing a more natural glow throughout the room.

Zosar watched the trio. His eyes kept a diligent watch on the BellKeys around their necks. *Those BellKeys must be mine! Used with my own power source, why the possibilities will be endless! Everything will be mine!* He felt a nip at his ear and noticed Noir who was pecking at him, *Excuse me! Ours for the taking.* His palms itched with anticipation. Rubbing them on his robe with glee, he plotted the downfall of the BellKeepers.

"Thank you, Zosar. This will suit us perfectly. What a help you have already become!" complimented Ashlar. "But, where is it that you reside?"

"Just a short distance farther down in this tunnel."

"Is there anything you or Noir need there?"

Besides those lovely trinkets you wear? Zosar wanted to say but instead he said, "Noir and I are perfectly comfortable in our humble abode. We like to live simply."

"As you wish but please let me know if there is anything we can do to make you more comfortable. We want you to know that you are appreciated," Ashlar, always the polite hostess, replied.

Easy, trusting fools! With a deep gracious-like bow Zosar assured them, "It is truly my pleasure to be a part of this great act upon our beloved forest."

Modie was defiant. He scrunched his face up tight and waved one hand towards the wall where he would sleep. The envisioned tunnel appeared.

He relaxed his stance and looked up at his parents who gazed at him with tolerance.

"Okay, Modie," Jamar said as he rubbed the top of his son's head, "You can keep this one, but where does it lead?"

"Yes! It just goes outside up on the mountain." Joyously, Modie rushed over to go through his new tunnel.

"No, Modie." Ashlar pointed towards his sleeping area. "You are staying inside."

Modie pulled aside the ivy vines and crawled up into his bed. Lying down on a petal-filled pillow, his last thought before sleep overtook him was, "I wonder what is a dead end?"

CHAPTER 9

One-Eye Zosar

"What is a dead end?"

Her eyes feeling heavy and blonde curls in a chaotic mess, Maddie asked her brother, Dylan, who was sitting at the kitchen table, the question that plagued her dreams throughout the night.

As Dylan devoured his breakfast, he glanced up at his sister. "Dead end means you can't go farther or you are being stopped from doing something. Why?"

Reaching for a bowl in the cabinet so she could make some cereal, Maddie replied, "I don't know. I was just thinking about it when I woke up. Are Mom and Dad awake yet?"

"Yeah, they had to go into work early and wanted me to remind you that you need to stay home after school. Guess they want to talk about yesterday. So, what was that all about, Maddie?"

She shrugged her shoulders and put her bowl now filled with cereal and milk on the table. After sitting down and taking a big bite of the sugary substance, she looked at her brother wondering if he would just laugh and tease her. She decided not to take the chance and replied, "Nothing much. Just another one of those things."

"Uh huh, and the story of the BellKeepers in the woods? Was that just another one of those things?"

"Yep, just a story." She got up and rinsed her bowl, and placed it in the dishwasher. "I am going to get ready for school now."

"This isn't over, Maddie. Mom and Dad are going to want more of an explanation than that," offered Dylan, who noticed a big smile on her face as she exited the kitchen. Dylan muttered, "I don't trust that look!"

You are right, Dylan. It isn't over! I am going to find proof about the BellKeepers right after school. Then everyone will have to believe me. With the plan of action firmly planted in her mind, she raced up the stairs to her room. *I so love an adventure!*

"I so love an adventure," Modie thought as he stretched and rose to greet the new day.

Scrambling out of his ivy-covered bed, Modie saw the note that his parents left for him on the stone table. It was written on a slate tablet with a quill that was fashioned as a writing tool then dipped in red berry ink.

> *Dear Son,*
>
> *We have gone to check on the forest. Please stay in the mountain until we return.*
>
> *Love, Mom and Dad*

"Perfect, I can now check out this mountain. Maybe I will be able to find proof about yesterday. Then my parents will have to listen to me."

Modie hustled through the tunnel that he just made. On all fours he proceeded to crawl through the helter-skelter tunnel knowing it was going to take him to the surface where he could see the entire forest on his own. Seeing the daylight ahead, he moved faster in anticipation.

He poked his head through the exit and checked out the surroundings to make sure it was safe. Safe from what, he was not sure but his parents had taught him to be careful.

His dirt-smudged face grinned when he saw the beautiful view. He climbed out and he stood tall with his hands on his hips, chest out. This was his Kingdom and he was the Ruler. The Mighty Modie he is called by his royal subjects. He stood outside and could see for miles around. He could see the LaHiere Village and his people coming awake. He saw the bridge that crossed the river swaying slightly with the morning breeze. From there, he saw the meadow that now had statuesque tulips surrounding the perimeter. By being outside, he could see B.B. that he healed the day before coming out to feed on the newly grown grass in the meadow. Outside is where . . .

"Oh no! I am supposed to be staying inside." Modie thought as he remembered his parents' note.

Modie went back into his exit hole, where he reclined half his body down and felt the cool earth as it touched his belly. He then propped his head on his hands to justify in his mind that he was still *in* the mountain.

Suddenly, a flashing light within the forest moving towards Bellmaur Peak caught Modie's attention. Scooting a bit more forward and quickly glancing back to see if he was still *in* the mountain—and his toes still hidden in the hole—Modie stretched his neck to watch the progress of the intriguing light.

Zosar with his ever present sidekick, Noir, on his shoulder, approached the entrance to Bellmaur Peak, unaware that he was being spied upon by the Mighty Modie.

Modie held his BellKey with one hand and brought it to his mouth and spoke into it, for yet again, he imagined he was in the battle zone. "Whoop, whoop sound the alarm, men! Code Red, Code Red! We have a breach on the south entrance. Stand by and hold your weapons while I take in the situation. Stand by! Beep!"

After placing his BellKey back in position on his chest, Modie made his way back down his tunnel to the family chambers. He checked out his living space and made note that all was clear there. Crouching through the key hole entrance, he went in the right tunnel. Then he hugged walls inching his way along as he informed his men of his progress.

"All clear in the right tunnel. I am almost in position of the south entrance, over."

Mighty Modie moved slowly and made it to the end of the right tunnel with no resistance. Peaking his head around the corner, he noted the presence of the enemy.

"Men, it is as I feared. Our worse nightmare come true! We have been invaded by the One-Eye Zosar and his knight Noir the Black Bird. They are armed. I repeat! They are armed with the Staff of Death. It appears they are heading down the Dead End tunnel. I am going to follow them. This is Mighty Modie, your Ruler. Over and out."

Modie followed Zosar and Noir—making sure he kept a safe distance away. He had to stay alert and focus on this mission. He kept control of his thoughts, which was a struggle for Modie knew that Noir could pick up his mind patterns if he was not careful.

Standing with his back against the wall, Modie watched the

intruders stop. They could not go farther for it was a dead end.

Modie whispered into his BellKey, "Men, we now know what a dead end is. We have our enemy cornered. They will have to stand and fight me in order to get by! Hey! Wait a second. They are looking around." Suddenly, Modie's eyes widened, "The enemy just walked right through the wall!"

Fascinated, Modie walked up to the Dead End wall. He checked out the other sides of the tunnel comparing it to the wall in front of him. It looked real enough. As Modie put a hand out to touch it, his fingers encountered a cold gel-like substance that his entire hand disappeared through. He pulled his hand back and watched the wall wiggle in response to his actions.

"We have a decoy man. I am going in. Stand by."

His heart racing with excitement, Modie entered the illusion. On the other side, his silhouette could be seen as he pressed forward with his hands outstretched. Tiny fingertips breached the barrier first. As his hands clawed through the unknown, the delicate membrane broke. With a final step forward, Modie gulped in much needed air. He looked back and watched the Dead End wall wobble back and forth. He even could see through the wall to the tunnel beyond.

"That was like walking through a bubble and I can see back through it! I have never seen anything like this before! Why is this here?"

Modie notified his troops. "I'm in the enemy camp. I can hear the One-Eye Zosar's voice just ahead. I am proceeding with caution. We are still in a Code Red situation!"

Zosar's voice brought Modie to a deep tunnel cave formed by an underground river that flowed through the limestone rock. The scenic wonderland opened to stalactites and stalagmites which adorned the cave's ceiling and floors. Walls were etched with eerie formations, some with symbols carved generations ago.

Seeing the score of bats roosting at the uppermost area of the cavern, Modie smiled in approval. "Thanks for the back-up men. Stay in formation and be prepared for the first wave on my command."

The single bat in the lead saluted Mighty Modie, his commander, and winked. *"General Alucard and troops are at your service, Sir."* Alu announced as he and the others fell into the game Modie created.

A grinning Modie stood at attention and saluted Alu.

Thinking that this was still all a game, Modie gazed down from the hidden cavity he was in and watched the enemy's activities.

He watched Zosar, who was hauling a large black cauldron to the pool of water that disappeared through a wall. Zosar dipped the iron pot into the water while Noir squawked loudly.

"I do not understand why you are complaining, Noir. You were the one who used the blue mist on that little BellKeeper. You know that you cannot do that when there are witnesses let alone another BellKeeper in the area. You were stopped so admit your defeat and carry on." Zosar hauled the water-filled cauldron to his table.

"Though all is not lost, Noir." He reassured his feathered friend, who was perched at the end of a table.

"If anything, our actions have brought those BellKeepers out into the open where they are now vulnerable. We just have to begin again with this water that feeds the LaHiere Village River," Zosar said. Taking his staff, Zosar put the crystal jewel into the water and stirred gradually making the water turn blue.

"Noir, go out into the forest and bring me some twigs. Three different sizes. We have to have a back-up plan in case things do not go our way again." And as an afterthought, "Oh, and bring me a living flower. It will be the perfect test subject."

Cawing his agreement, Noir soared off in flight through the tunnel exiting into the forest.

Modie could not make sense of what he heard. What did Zosar mean that he brought us into the open? And what is that stuff he is making?

Modie decided to get a bit closer edging his way out from the cavity. A stone dislodged from the earthen floor and started to bounce down making pinging noises with its descent.

Halting his stirring motions, Zosar took a look around.

"Uh oh!" Modie said. Looking up at Alu, he called for help.

Alu let go of his hold. Glorious wings spanned out and his black furry body glided down through the air drawing Zosar's attention away from where Modie was hiding. Using its fingers within the wing membrane, Alu was able to lift and thrust its way around Zosar's body.

Irritated, Zosar swung his arms around to avoid contact with the furry beast.

"Meddlesome creatures! You are just like the Pilutars." Watching as the bat settled itself back in his roosting position, Zosar then concentrated on the formula he was creating.

With a sigh of relief, Modie sent his thanks up to his soldier. Alucard, smiling, wiggled his pointed ears in response.

Modie decided that maybe he should wait until Zosar left before going down to explore. He settled back wondering what his adventure was going to bring him next.

CHAPTER 10

General Alu to the Rescue

Noir entered the cavern with his beak full of dead twigs and a flower clutched within his claws. He dropped the flower in front of Zosar (who was still busy stirring the potion) and completed his flight with ease landing next to the pot once again. After arranging the three twigs side by side, he then looked at his master with expectation.

The potion swirled within the black cauldron. Wispy drifts of blue steam rose in the air. Dancing, the haze swirled around Zosar who brought his nose to it and sniffed. The scent brought pure satisfaction to his face. With a push of his hands, the aroma went to Noir who cawed his delight.

Zosar praised his feathered friend as he picked up the tulip. "The Pilutars' sacred flower, a tulip. Excellent specimen, Noir. This delicate beauty is the perfect substitute. They may have brought life back, but I have the power to end it once and for all!" He dipped the flower into the solution and pulled it back out. As the life force drained from the wax-like petal tulip, Zosar laughed in triumph.

"Ready the twigs, Noir. They will be our last resort."

Pecking at each end making a razor-sharp point, Noir then handed the trio, one by one, to Zosar who coated each end with the poison chemical being careful not to encounter the liquid himself.

Zosar went to the pool of water that fed the river and washed his hands. "Look at this water source, Noir. Do you realize how simple it will be to send our poison to the townspeople? They would never know what hit them. It really is disgusting how good we are! We will have to think on this possibility later. Right now we need to let this batch ferment a short time. Let us go above and check on the status of the BellKeepers. Things have been too quiet and I don't trust that interloping family."

Modie sat frozen in his spot even though the coast was clear. His breath came out in short rapid spurts. What started as an adventure became a horrific discovery. Zosar and Noir are the ones responsible for the fatal acts upon the forest and now they are plotting to attack the village where Maddie lives!

Shaking his head sharply, Modie decided he needed to focus on this new mission knowing that this time it was not a game.

He quickly left his hiding place, not worrying about the amount of noise he made. Time was of the essence, because the enemy could be back any minute. Slipping and sliding, Modie made his way down the different rock formations. He came to the table that had the black kettle on it and stood on tiptoe trying to see the top. He was just too short. He thought that he could pull himself up, so he stretched his arms high above his head. His fingertips struggled to get a grasp. It was just too high.

Sighing, Modie closed his eyes and concentrated. A vine,

which sprouted from the ground, spiraled on top of the table. Modie climbed the vine to see what was on the table top. Set before him were the three twigs that he saw Zosar dipping in the blue chemical. There were several empty tubes and other paraphernalia cluttered the table top along with the large black kettle.

"Three twigs? Why would Zosar want three twigs as a back up?" Thinking to himself, three, *hmmm, poison chemicals, three, back up. . . .*

"No!" Modie yelled. "He is going to use those on us, the BellKeepers. I have got to warn Mom and Dad but first I will need proof. I know they won't believe me if I don't this time."

Modie looked around and found a small vial with a tiny cork top. Perfect!

"Hurry, hurry! Time is wasting!" Alucard warned.

"Okay, I am almost there." Modie dipped the tube into the liquid that bubbled and hissed on contact and was able to get the evidence he needed.

"Time is up!" Zosar's voice in the tunnel reached Modie's pointed ears.

"Huh?" Jerking his body towards the sound, Modie caused the chemical to slosh over the still opened tube. A searing pain hit him in the side. Gasping, Modie watched the blue liquid eat away a small area of his skin. He heard Zosar's voice coming closer, so he knew he was out of time. The only exit out was where Zosar was coming from. He was trapped!

Modie blocked out the pain and grabbed the cork and sealed the vial shut. He held it firmly within his fist and leaped off the table executing a perfect somersault in the air. Upon landing he concentrated on the wall ahead, throwing his arm out. The exit tunnel appeared as planned—leading out of the mountain into the safety of the forest.

Modie glanced up to his friends and gave a brief parting salute.

"Take care, Modie. We will back you up if ever necessary." Then Alu moved his head and looked behind Modie. *"Oh, no!"*

Whirling around, Modie's gaze encountered Zosar, who stood just a short distance away holding his staff. Noir, traditionally, sat upon Zosar's shoulder, head jutted out looking as if he was ready to charge. Zosar's dark gaze held absolute fury.

Protectively, Modie held the vial close to his chest with both hands.

"Well, well! Isn't this interesting, Noir? We have a trespasser not to mention a thief. Tell me, boy, what was your name again?"

Though his heart was racing, Modie stood proud. "As you well know, my name is Modie. I am a BellKeeper."

"A BellKeeper you say? Not for long!" With a fluid motion, Zosar raised his staff slamming the end tip on the floor sharply. A humming sound invaded the room. The clear crystal vibrated and turned blue. Whipping it forward, he pointed it at Modie. Instantly a beam flashed outward engulfing Modie's wrists. With a flick of the staff, Zosar sent Modie's cuffed arms over his head.

Modie struggled and tried to break the hold, but it was iron tight. He felt a tugging on his arms and was lifted into the air by the beam Zosar controlled. Looking up, he saw that the vial was still protected in the palm of one hand. But, as he looked down he saw the ground move as he was led to hover over the black cauldron.

Modie watched the steam rise wrapping itself around his body. A familiar hand formed and paused near his BellKey.

"Watch and learn, Noir," said Zosar as he twisted his staff causing the beam to tighten its hold on Modie.

"You won't get away with this, Zosar. My parents will stop you if I can't."

"I beg to differ with you, dear boy. I am already getting away with this. Oh, look, Noir! Our little BellKeeper seems to have been playing with the chemical," Zosar said as he spied the lesion festering on Modie's side. "Didn't your parents tell you not to play with poison?"

Modie was feeling the pain from his wound and the pain radiated up his side. He groaned, but yet again blocked the agony he was feeling. "What do you want, Zosar?"

"I want you to relinquish the BellKey." Zosar paused and glanced at the pot. "Or die!"

"What does relinquish mean?"

"GIVE ME THE KEY!" Zosar roared.

A loud fluttering sound echoed in the chamber. The bats in the famous "V" formation soared to Modie's rescue. The lead bat, Alucard, flew into the beam sacrificing its body as it now absorbed the power that held Modie captive.

"Alu! No!" Modie screamed as he watched his friend deflect the beam from him. Upon Alu's impact, Modie was instantly free. His tiny body plunged to the waiting liquid. Swooping down, two of the night-winged creatures settled themselves beneath Modie's feet. Balancing him on their backs, they carried him off from a near death.

Furious, Zosar roared at Noir. "Catch him! Do not let him escape!"

"I am BAT FLYING!" Flexing his legs, he let his body flow with the movement of his bat friends. Still being cautious with his prized possession, he guided the bats to Zosar. He took his BellKey off from around his neck and swung the chain in circles like a lasso. A golden halo formed that spun rapidly. Focusing his energy on Zosar's staff, Modie struck it with the spiraling BellKey making Zosar's hand jerk from the force. The beam retracted back and Alu was set free.

"Perfect!" Modie cheered as he guided his bats to the exit where the Dead End wall awaited.

"NO, NO! He has the vial!" Zosar screamed, "STOP HIM!" Agitated, Zosar dropped the staff. He ran to the tunnel exit, slipping and sliding in a comic display on the wet limestone rocks.

Seeing the Dead End wall ahead, Modie said, "We are almost there—keep going, keep going." Knowing that Zosar and Noir were right behind him, he encouraged the flight—loving the feel of the air that pulled at his face from the speed they attained.

Suddenly, Modie heard the cawing voice of Noir. *"You will not get away."* Lunging Noir nipped at one of the bats' legs making Modie go off balance. Modie could not stop his momentum and went flying head first through the Dead End wall. He hit the side wall which knocked the vial from Modie's grasp, sending it crashing to the floor. The blue poison seeped into the dirt floor.

As he went through the wall, Modie did the only thing he could think of.

He yelled, "Moooommmmieee!"

Standing at the mouth of the cave, Ashlar continued to collect the berries and nuts she found there. Jamar was still in the forest trying to find evidence of any wrongdoing.

When Modie's cry reached her, she dropped the collection of nourishment. Ashlar clutched her BellKey in panic allowing it to lead her to her son who clearly was in trouble. For in trouble he was, she could feel it.

She ran down the Dead End tunnel and encountered Modie, who was faced down on the dirt floor. The menacing Zosar, with Noir on his shoulder, stood over her son.

"Modie!" Dropping to her knees, she lifted her son up to her lap. She stroke his forehead and rocked back and forth in the timeless mother motion. "Wake up, son. Come on, that's it."

Eyes fluttering, Modie's red gaze lit upon his mother. "Mom!"

Ashlar, glaring at Zosar, demanded—"What happened here? What did you do to my son?"

"Why absolutely nothing, dear!" Zosar replied with Noir cawing his agreement.

When Modie heard Zosar's voice, he scrambled out of his mother's arms. Ashlar held her hand out to her son who took it in his grasp, pulling himself up. Immediately Modie hid behind his mother.

"Nothing, you say? Then why is my son hiding from you?"

Before Zosar could say his piece, Modie launched into his rendition of the events that happened to him.

"It is them Mom," accused Modie as he pointed his finger at the twosome. "They are the ones who killed the forest. They have a chemical! His stick has this beam that tried to kill me but Alu, the bat, saved my life. Then I was bat flying!" Modie's face changed to one of excitement. "I was soaring through the air and whack! I stopped the beam from hurting Alu."

"Modie," Ashlar's doubting voice warned.

"Mom, I am telling you the truth! There is a chemical room," Modie exclaimed.

"Modie! There are no chemicals here," Ashlar replied, throwing her arms out in disgust.

"No, no wait! All we have to do is walk through that wall and oh! I have proof!"

"What proof, Modie?" Ashlar asked with a sigh.

Seeing the cork to the vial of poison on the ground, Zosar immediately placed his foot on top of it, blocking it from anyone's view. Then he said, "Yes, dear Modie. What proof could you possibly have that would give credence to this preposterous story?"

Looking at Zosar, Modie said confidently, "The vial with the blue chemical!" He held out his hand only to realize that his hand was empty. "Oh no, I must of dropped it!" Modie looked around and tried to find the missing item. He felt faint from hitting his head, so he struggled to stay standing. He held his forehead and tried to stop his head from spinning. Thoughts raced throughout his mind, but he was unable to focus on the one he needed—the proof which was right there before them. The Dead End wall.

With a sigh, Ashlar helped steady her son on his feet. "As usual I seem to owe you an apology, Zosar. But, this fabricated story of Modie's still does not explain why I found my son on the ground."

"I am afraid that is my fault, Madam. Noir and I saw young Modie here traveling down this tunnel. We were so afraid of his safety that we followed him. We asked him to stop before he could get hurt. Well, I am sad to say that we startled him. Modie jumped, called out to you before hitting his head on the wall. And for that I need to apologize to you, my good woman. It was never our intention to harm this young man." Zosar explained and almost believing it himself.

"Well, that explains that. Zosar, if you will excuse us, we need to leave you in peace. Modie, come with me!"

"But, Mom—"

Ashlar took Modie by the ear, and gently tugged. "Now!"

"Yes, ma'am." Modie walked away to the sounds of Noir's cackling laughter.

In a hushed whisper, Zosar spoke to his assistant, "We are going to have to follow them. That was a tad too easy. I keep feeling like we forgot something." Pulling his staff out, Zosar and Noir followed the two.

CHAPTER 11

A BellKeeper Is Dying

Back in their personal chambers, Ashlar continued to lecture Modie. "This is the second time in as many days that you told stories to justify yourself. This is not acceptable behavior. Are you having problems adjusting to our job here? Has it become too much for you? What is it, Modie? I need you to talk to me!"

"Mom, I wish you would believe me. I have not lied to you once! It is Zosar." A sharp pain pierced his side once again. Groaning in agony, Modie clutched his side and he turned away from his mother.

"What is it, Modie? What have you done to yourself?" She walked up behind him and placed her hands softly on his shoulders. "Did you hurt yourself when you fell?" She peeled his hands away from his body, and bent down to see what the problem was. Evidence of the pain Modie was feeling shook Ashlar deeply. Charred fur exposed a raw sore that looked as if it were a severe burn.

She gasped in shock. Grasping Modie firmly, she turned him around to face her. She crouched down to his level and looked him square in the eye. "Modie! What in the world happened to you?"

"Mom, I told you. It was the chemicals in the room behind the Dead End wall." Remembering that he did not actually tell his mom about the wall, he continued, "You can go back and walk through that wall and see it for yourself." Modie replied weakly. "That will prove what I say is true." His strength was draining now that the adrenaline had worn off from his escapades.

Ashlar stared at Modie and began to believe. Going over everything that Modie had claimed in her mind, Ashlar came to realize that her son had been telling the truth all this time. The brown door, Noir the crow, Zosar and chemicals. Everything has been right in front of them this whole time! So many questions were now answered but the main one still laid empty.

Why?

Ashlar guided her son to his sleeping area and helped him get comfortable by putting him down and covering him with a moss blanket.

"Modie, I need you to use your BellKey and heal yourself. This is going to be difficult and will drain your energy. But, it must be done and soon before an infection sets in."

Modie wrapped his hand around his BellKey and with his mother's help placed it on his side. A delicate golden glow surrounded their bodies.

As the luminescence of the BellKey's magic slowly ebbed away, Ashlar brushed a tender kiss on her son's check. "Rest now. No harm will come to you."

"Where are you going?" Modie asked weakly.

"Right now I am going to contact the Ancient Ones and inform them of what has occurred. Then we will see."

Zosar, who was in the tunnel outside of the BellKeepers chambers eavesdropping, knew that he was caught. "Noir, go to the lab and collect a piece of hallow bamboo. Put a single twig inside it and By the Tulips! Be careful not to drop anything. I will meet you on the other side of the Dead End wall. Hurry!" As Noir flew off, Zosar followed muttering to himself, "I knew we forgot something! Encroaching family!"

Ashlar walked over to their table and sat on the stone stool. She put her arms on the table, hands flat against the cool surface and sat perfectly straight, eyes closed. With deep, even breaths she went in to a trance-like sleep. Using her BellKey's energy, she felt her inner self lift and soar in flight.

Walking through a foggy haze, Ashlar stopped in front of an ornate podium that was inscribed with the Celtic-like cross. Vapors swirled in front of her as the Ancient Ones walked through, presenting themselves in the single file row. Immediately, Ashlar dropped to one knee and then stood in a sign of respect.

"You have risked much by summoning us, Ashlar of the BellKeepers. You have opened the Veil and left yourself vulnerable."

"I offer my humble apologies, sirs. The need was great for we, the BellKeepers, have encountered a dilemma and seek your wisdom."

Ashlar spoke of the treachery and deceit that they had experienced. Her concern for Modie was evident and she wondered what steps they needed to take to amend and protect.

"I feel as if we have failed the Pilutars in the quest given to us." Ashlar ended with her head bowed.

"Failing is not an option, Ashlar. You were blinded by a powerful force. We have sensed this familiar presence for some time, but we were never able to pinpoint the cause or reason. Now your eyes are open. Call Jamar and together you two can investigate. Go to the Dead End wall that you spoke of."

"But what of Modie? Should we leave him alone?"

"Your son, the Third BellKeeper, is safe for now. He has great strength of will. We have chosen well with you and your family. Jamar's BellKey represents strength and power—to complete life. Yours offers the love, security and cherishing needed to survive, while young Modie has the ability to heal and bring joyful laughter to those around him. His oneness with the forest is astounding. All three of you have given more of your personal natures than we ever deemed possible. Now, go and seek your husband. All will come to pass that was meant to be."

As the Ancient Ones faded back, Ashlar turned and walked away.

Gasping in fresh air, Ashlar became one with herself. She took in her surroundings as her mind re-oriented itself.

After checking on Modie, who was resting quietly, she headed for the key hole exit. She entered the right tunnel and raised her BellKey to the family's entrance. A shimmering light curtain filled the doorway. "You are secure now, son. Only your father and I will be able to get through. I will be back." She whispered knowing that her message would reach him in his dreams.

Striding purposely, Ashlar headed for Dead End wall, calling Jamar with her BellKey as she went.

On the other side of the wall Zosar watched Ashlar approach. "That's it. Come just a bit closer. Yes!"

Bringing the bamboo chute to his mouth, he aimed for the side of her throat. He blew the poisoned twig through the wall and it shot through and hit its target, embedding itself.

Ashlar felt the slight sting on her neck and slapped at it. Her mind became fuzzy. "What was I trying to do? Oh, yes—wait for Jamar—Jamar—need you now—so dark—can't think." She grabbed her head and tried to stop the spinning. A black void entered her mind and in sweet oblivion she crumbled to the dirt floor.

Meanwhile, Jamar, who was standing in the middle of a grassy field, crouched down and examined a burnt strip of grass. The long rectangular shape was completely at odds with the rest of the area. Touching his fingers along the infertile strip, he rubbed them together and sniffed the odor.

"How strange," he murmured.

He looked around, but did not see anything that could have caused this reaction to the otherwise thriving area. There were some forest animals at the edge of the clearing. How he wished Modie were here to talk to them.

His BellKey rang startling him from his thoughts. He grasped it and heard Ashlar's call for him. A sinking feeling came when he heard the distorted words that followed.

He ran out of the clearing. A majestic buck leaped in front of him blocking his way. Snorting and pawing the ground, the bold animal tossed his head in an invitation. So Jamar leaped on to the stag's back and wrapped his arms around the muscular neck.

Swiftly the buck carried Jamar through the forest, racing towards the mountain. He tried repeatedly to reach his wife through his BellKey, but there was no response. Truly panicked now he urged the magnificent animal to go faster. All thoughts of the strip of dead grass are gone from his mind.

Zosar was completely overjoyed. He clapped his hands and said, "One down, two to go. Now, all I need is her BellKey." His hand encountered the Dead End wall. Pushing through, Zosar went for the BellKey that was cradled on the body of the fallen BellKeeper. An anguished cry stopped him from allowing his hand to penetrate the final layer.

"ASHLAR!!!" Screaming, Jamar raced towards the prone figure on the dirt floor.

The tunnel seemed to stretch endlessly as Jamar ran to his wife. Skidding the rest of the way on his knees, Jamar frantically gathered her in his arms, holding her close. Her breathing was so shallow and face deathly white.

A tormented moan echoed, "No, no!"

Bringing his head to her chest, Jamar listened for a heartbeat. There was a painfully slow thud. He stood, carrying his wife in his arms, her body hanging limp like a rag doll. Confused, he looked around trying to decide what to do. His beloved wife, his life-mate was dying. She needed to be healed.

Ashlar needed Modie.

Her son, the Third BellKeeper.

CHAPTER 12

Jamar's BellKey Seized

Jamar ducked through the entrance of their chambers, mindful of his wife he was nurturing in his arms. He vaguely noted the whisper-thin veil he went through. Briefly, he wondered why that was present. The veil disappeared along with the thought as soon as he saw his son resting.

"Modie! We need you!"

Jamar made his way to their bed, gently putting Ashlar down on the soft tulip petals. As he brushed his hands along the sides of her face and neck, he encountered the protruding twig. Puzzled, he turned her face to the side. The tiny piece of wood was embedded in the main vein that traveled down her neck. He reached for the splinter-like piece planning on pulling it out.

"No! Don't touch it, Dad!" Modie yelled.

Jamar looked at his son who now stood by his side. "Why? You can tell it is hurting her."

"Just let me check her first, Dad."

Bowing his head, Jamar stepped aside but still hovered over Modie, who was standing by the side of his parents' bed. Modie ran his hands lightly over his mother's body.

"Dad, she has been poisoned. It is now running through her veins." With tears running down both father and son's faces, Modie stated the obvious. "She is dying. It is Zosar. He is the one doing this. I found his chemical room, Dad."

"Zosar did this?" Jamar asked in disbelief.

"Yes! There is a room behind the Dead End wall—"

"Modie! We do not have time for the explanation now. I do understand what you have said, but right now we need to worry about your mother. Can you heal her? Can you stop this poison you speak of in time?"

"I can try."

"It will take everything you have! You know that, don't you? Once you start you cannot break away because then surely we will lose her. You must not ever let her go." Jamar's eyes focused on his son. He grasped Modie's shoulders, "So, again, I ask you, can you do this?"

Modie stared into his father's eyes and knew that this was his biggest challenge of all. "I will do everything I can to heal her, Dad. And I promise to not let her go."

Torn between pride for his son and worry over his wife, Jamar stood, quickly clasping his son in a strong hold. His arms wrapping around the slight body that had taken on so many responsibilities while other Seed Cycle Pilutars are out playing and discovering.

"I love you, Modie." Jamar stepped aside moving several feet away.

After taking a deep soulful breath, Modie faced his mother who lay blissfully unaware. Her body, looking so peaceful lying on the tulip petals, was so at odds with the turmoil inside her body.

Modie crawled up next to his mother—a beautiful scene of a mother and son curled up sleeping.

"Remember, Dad—beware of Zosar!" After warning his

dad, Modie relaxed his mind and focused entirely upon the woman who had nurtured him since birth. The golden glow enclosed the two cradling bodies, pulsing life with each halo beam.

This was not like when Modie was injured. His was but a surface wound. Ashlar's is life threatening, so Modie needed to take her to a peaceful place where no interference can happen. Though his subconscious was completely aware of his father pacing and worrisome thoughts, he was not allowed to address it. He must focus on his mother only.

Ashlar's life force was transported to another dimension; one in the clouds. There Modie was able to give of himself, allowing his gift to flow through her veins and fight the evil that was betraying her life.

Like a picture within a picture, Modie and Ashlar stood in a healing realm holding each other's hands. In front of them they were able to see Jamar, who repeatedly moved to go to the bed holding his wife and son.

"*He is a strong man, your Father, but he is very vulnerable now.*"

"*This is how it must be for now, Mother. Your shell of a body was dying.*"

"*You are a brave boy and I am so very proud of you. Your father and I owe you a deep apology for doubting you.*" Looking at Modie's downcast face, Ashlar wondered what the problem was. "*Modie?*"

"*Dad does not know everything, Mom. He knows to watch out for Zosar, but that is it.*"

"*What?*"

"*There wasn't any time! I needed to bring you here without any delay.*"

Turning, she gazed at her husband. With her BellKey, she tried to warn him.

"*He isn't going to hear you, Mom. You are still healing. The poison in your body is very deadly and even now is in a fatal battle with me.*"

Gasping, Ashlar clutched her heart. Pointing to the vision before them, she whispered "*Zosar!*"

Modie felt dreadful as he watched the scene before him knowing that there was not one thing he could do to warn his father.

Cautiously Zosar, with Noir on his shoulder, peered around the corner to the entrance of the BellKeepers' chambers. Seeing Jamar's back to him and Modie lying with his mother brought a sickening smile to Zosar's face. As he noticed the golden haze that surrounded the two BellKeepers, Zosar knew what was transpiring.

He glanced up at Noir and whispered, "Now is the perfect time. Why, look at the all mighty BellKeepers now. One is dying, thanks to my genius, the other is grieving and Modie, the most irritating of all, is trying to heal *his little Mommy.*" The last he said in a sneer. "Now this is the way you should have done it the first time. Watch and learn my feathered friend because the BellKeepers are going to fall."

Taking his staff, Zosar pointed the crystal to the ground. In slow circle, Zosar spun the staff causing the stone to glow making a blue mist. He pointed the staff at Jamar and the blue haze responded to Zosar's bidding. Slithering and weaving on the floor, it headed towards Jamar's feet.

"Oh no! Jamar!" Ashlar cried.

"Dad! Look out!" Modie yelled in turn.

"Hang on to her, son. Don't let her go. You are doing so well." Jamar offered his praise to Modie not knowing that the real danger was in the room with him.

The blue mist wrapped around Jamar's feet, then rapidly around his legs.

"By the Tulips!" Jamar cried out.

The mist continued around Jamar's body trapping his arms to his side. Jamar struggled and tried to break the hold but it was no use. He was held too tight! The energy seeped from his body, and he could feel his mind drifting.

The blue mist formed into a hand, its fingers wiggled then

reached for the BellKey. Swiftly, it tightened the chain around Jamar's neck as a show of hatred before plucking the BellKey away from his possession. The golden-encased BellKey glinted as it rocked back and forth, swinging from its chain. Zosar watched the movement with greedy delight as he made his entrance and reached for the BellKey.

Ashlar and Modie watched the events in what appeared to be slow motion.

"Modie! Release me! You must let me go and help your father. I am begging you to just let me go!"

Torn between the two loyalties, Modie saw the BellKey in Zosar's hand. His father's BellKey in Zosar's control would cause unbelievable destruction. If he let go of his mother she would die.

With tears streaming down his face, Modie looked at his mother. "I can't let you go, Mommy. I love you—I can't let you go—Daddy said to never let you go."

Bringing her son close to her side, Ashlar sighed deep. "So be it. Let us hope that we will be able to undo any damage that will be done."

Reverently, Zosar felt the gold chain touch his palm. He wrapped his fingers around the BellKey and felt the power absorb into his being.

Zosar brought his staff to the ground ordering the mist to retract. The mist obeyed and upon his release, Jamar's legs buckled sending him to his knees in defeat.

CHAPTER 13

The Staff of Death

W hat has happened?" asked the now groggy Jamar.

Ashlar and Modie finished telling him all that had transpired before Ashlar was poisoned. In shock, Jamar had collapsed on one of the stone stools, his head in his hands. Still weak, Ashlar and Modie sat beside him watching him with concern.

"We cannot dwell on what has been done but what we need to do now. The forest will respond to the BellKey in Zosar's power so I am sure everything is undone. Goodness knows what else he has planned. Zosar will not waste any time." Ashlar reasoned.

Jamar slammed his fist on the table. "By the Tulips! We have to get that BellKey back and put a stop to that man. If we only knew why he is doing this! Well, I am the one who will seek out Zosar and retrieve my BellKey!"

"Jamar, be reasonable! Your anger will rule your heart. He will know why you are coming. Then he will take great steps to prevent you from succeeding. Possible steps that I do not want to think of. There has to be another way."

"I am small and can hide fast. I can do it." A soft voice offered.

"No, son. You have done so much for us already—besides you are still weak from healing your mother."

"Dad, I have been in Zosar's chemical room. You have not. Like I said, I am small plus I have General Alucard, the bat I told you about."

"He is right, Jamar, as much as it pains me to say. Our son is the one that needs to find the BellKey," Ashlar said.

"We don't even know that the BellKey is in this room you have been telling me about. He could be wearing it. Then what would Modie do?" Jamar asked his wife.

Modie spoke up before his mother could reply, "It has to be in Zosar's chambers, Dad. Remember the Ancients said that the BellKeys would protect themselves. Zosar would not be able to wear the BellKey for long. The only safe place he would have is his room behind the Dead End wall."

Jamar knew he was fighting a losing battle. He looked at his son who had grown up so quickly. "How did you get so wise so soon?"

"By watching you and mom. Everyone makes mistakes, Dad. We just have to learn from them at least that is what you always say."

"Come here." Opening his arms wide, Jamar beckoned his child. Modie, scrambling off the stool, went into his father's arms, absorbing the feel of love and protection as they enclosed around him. "We are so very proud of you, Modie, so very proud."

Pulling away from his Dad, Modie looked at both of his parents. "Where should we meet after I get the BellKey?"

"How about in the meadow? It is right on the border of the forest. Then as soon as we have all three BellKeys we could

renew the forest immediately and deal with Zosar as a unit."
Jamar said.

Ashlar nodded her head in agreement. "Be careful, Modie.
We will wait for you there."

As Modie left his living area, Zosar and Noir were busy in their
own chambers. They had already destroyed the forest once
again but now the greed became stronger.

"Did I not tell you how brilliant I am? See, if you had used
the blue mist properly the first time we would have two Bell-
Keys now. Well, either way, I have saved us. Hold that chain
still, Noir! I just need to touch my crystal for a brief moment
on that BellKey."

Squawking, Noir ruffled his feathers and flapped his wings.

"Mind your words, bird. I do not have the patience for your
excuses. Keep it steady," said Zosar, who brought the crystal
closer to the BellKey, "That's it. Perfect!" The two touched
with a spark. Jamar's BellKey glowed bright then a small area
in the upper clasp dimmed to a dull brass color, contrasting
with the rest of the golden sheen.

"There! I have taken what I need for now." Zosar snatched
the BellKey from Noir's beak and laughed out loud. "If you
could only see me now, Flora!"

"Men, I have been through the trenches and it has been ugly.
My energy is low, but I have to go back into the enemy camp."
As Modie made his way back to the Dead End wall, he notified
his soldiers with his thoughts.

*"Mighty Modie, it is good to hear your voice. I can sense your weakness
of the body. Perhaps you should wait."* General Alucard responded.

"Life, sometimes, does not give you a choice. The One-Eye Zosar has my father's BellKey and it must be returned to him," said Modie, who added, "I need a status report of the area."

"Caution must be made. Your One-Eye Zosar is present along with Noir the Black Bird."

"And the BellKey?"

"Present and accounted for, sir. It was quite amusing, really. The BellKey burned the One-Eye Zosar. The bird had to fly and put it on a peg in the wall near the escape tunnel you made previously."

"Excellent! I am now through the wall and at the entrance. Stand by."

"At your command."

Modie maneuvered behind and around rock formations and made his way farther into the chamber. Lying on his belly, he used his arms and elbows to scoot his way to each point making sure to glance up at his troops for any signal of warning.

Then he crouched behind a stalagmite that was built up from the cavern's floor and saw that he was a few yards away from the BellKey and his tunnel. As Modie peaked from the other side of the rock, he saw Zosar and Noir making a new poison. Zosar, rubbing his hand, complained. "What good is that BellKey if I cannot touch it whenever I want to. That wretched item burned me! Does not matter. I will use it sparingly. But, now we shall concentrate on the townspeople."

Zosar placed his staff with the crystal burning an even brighter blue into the newly filled cauldron and stirred. "With this batch poured into the water source it will flow straight into the river, poisoning the LaHiere Village water supply. That should teach those supposed BellKeepers and let them know who is the powerful one here." He pulled his staff out of the steamy blue liquid and carried the cauldron to the pool of water.

Modie mumbled to himself, "I am really getting tired of making decisions. If this is what it takes to grow antennae then I don't want them."

He knew the decision that must be made. The BellKey would have to wait yet again. He moved out from behind the rock and stood out in the open.

"I am afraid I can't let you do that," said Modie in his best little man voice to Zosar's back.

Zosar's movement stopped. Slowly he placed the pot on the dirt ground and straightened his body. As he turned around, Noir squawked and flew to his shoulder.

"A little late for the warning, bird." Facing Modie, Zosar put his hands on his hips and laughed. The evil sound vibrated off the cavern's wall. Zosar's black eye bored into Modie. "Our little Mighty Modie is back," he said sarcastically. "I am really getting bored with these games. You really have no idea whom you are dealing with. Do you, little Pilutar?"

With a grand motion, Zosar peeled away the fabric covering his face and revealed two solid black eyes, a hawk-thin beak of a nose, long chin with a goatee. And with a final sweep, Zosar's head covering came off. His antennae sprang free from the black skullcap.

"Ancient One, Rasoz!" Modie immediately recognized him from the portraits in the Regent's castle. In an automatic reaction, Modie started to bow down on one knee only to stop. As Modie rose back up slowly, he realized that everything made sense now. Rasoz was the banished Ancient One!

"Ahhh, so the light has dawned. I can see it in your eyes. You, BellKeepers thought you were so very smart. HA! All this time everything was before you. If you have learned anything, learn this! Always look below the surface!"

"I still cannot let you harm the townspeople, Rasoz."

"How innocent and pure you are," Rasoz said in a droll

voice. "And just how do you think you can stop me?" He stepped around the poison-filled pot, bending down to pick it up.

"LIKE THIS!" Modie yelled and with a swift motion he used his Pilutar power, throwing his arm out and pointing to the pot. Thick ivy vines sprouted from the dirt floor and wrapped their leaves around the black cauldron. As the vine grew larger and larger, the pot shook and instantly tipped over, away from Rasoz's feet. Poisonous liquid poured out and seeped into the ground. Modie turned his attention to the pool of water that escaped through the cavern wall. Silently, he willed the wall to close off that area. Earth rumbled and a series of rocks took shape and tumbled into the water building a natural dam. Sucking in a deep breath through puckered lips, Modie directed the wall to absorb the water.

"I am impressed. Very quick thinking. You have saved your townspeople, at least for now. But, tell me, aren't you forgetting something?"

Modie turned and faced Rasoz who now stood in front of Modie's tunnel. "I never forget," Modie replied.

"Not even this?" With a flourish, Rasoz stretched out one arm, fist clasped close. As he opened his hand, the BellKey dropped down dangling from its chain.

"I would never forget that!" Looking up, Modie yelled, "NOW!"

Leading the way General Alucard and his troops swooped down screeching, flying into Rasoz's face. Some latched themselves on his head, pulling at his antennae, others thrashed at his robe.

He was startled by the unexpected attack, so Rasoz let go of the cherished BellKey. Before the BellKey could hit the ground Alucard caught it with his mouth and flew immediately over to Modie.

Fully intending on going through the tunnel he made earlier that day, Modie scrambled between Rasoz's legs which were still occupied by the bats. He stood and raised his head only to encounter Noir. Noir the Black Bird was blocking his way! With his black wings spread out, cawing his anger, Noir tried to peck at Modie to get him to drop the BellKey.

Some of his soldiers came to his aid offering a counter attack against Noir the Black Bird.

"Run, Modie! Run for the Dead End wall. We will hold them off as long as possible." Alu yelled.

"NOIR! FIND MY STAFF!" Running through the tunnel, Modie could hear the roar of Rasoz's displeasure. He anticipated the dreaded blue beam from Rasoz's staff to hit him at any moment, so he did a flying leap, feet first, through the Dead End wall. He made a smooth landing and went to take off again but was pulled back.

"Oh, no! The BellKey is stuck!" The chain was free but the BellKey was still inside the Dead End wall. The suction of the membrane was holding it tight and Modie tried to get the BellKey loose. But panic set in Modie's mind as Rasoz's yells were getting closer.

"I have to hide this BellKey. Rasoz is too close!" Modie thought. Quickly, Modie tucked the part of the chain that was free back into the Dead End wall.

Noir's cawing and Rasoz's pounding footsteps resounded off the walls. Modie ran to the exit for the forest straightway, calling for his mom with his BellKey.

"Mom! Mom! Zosar is really Rasoz the Ancient One!" Panting, Modie's little feet kept running, "I need help—I'm in the forest—I could not get dad's BellKey—it's hidden—getting tired—Rasoz is right behind me."

Standing in the meadow that was dead once again, Jamar and Ashlar waited for their son. Then jerking suddenly,

Ashlar grabbed a hold of her BellKey and heard her son's cries.

"Jamar! Zosar is actually Rasoz! Modie is in the forest and needs our help!" Ashlar grabbed Jamar by the arm and continued, "Jamar, he does not have the BellKey."

"I will go and get him. Tell Modie to hold on!" Jamar responded. As he ran into the forest, he yelled back at his wife, "Get ready for what we discussed. Call on the Ancient Ones and ask for some of the Royal Draugs. We have no choice now."

Breaking through the forest, the first blue lightning bolt struck a tree near where Modie was. He ducked low and continued on, darting in a zigzag motion.

Modie's BellKey flopped around on his back as he ran, glinting in the afternoon sunlight. Seeing the golden sparkle, Rasoz focused his next strike on the single BellKey. *"Single Bell-Key? Where is Jamar's BellKey?"* Rasoz thought. Yelling at Noir, Rasoz sent the black bird back into the mountain to look for the BellKey.

"The little fool must of dropped it or hidden it somewhere. FIND IT!" Rasoz, now frustrated and furious, brought his attention back to Modie who was getting farther away.

"YOU CAN NOT ESCAPE ME!" he roared.

As Modie looked back, he saw Rasoz raising his staff getting ready to strike again. He slammed the staff onto the ground and his bone-chilling laugh become one with the power that vibrated in the air. Another lightning bolt shot out, barely missing Modie yet again.

"MOM! DAD!" Modie's voice carried through the dead trees.

Rushing towards his son, Jamar yelled back, "I am here, Modie! You will be safe now!" He scooped his son up in his arms and backtracked to where his wife was anxiously waiting.

On the way, Jamar encountered a massive series of lightning which nipped at his footsteps. He continued since Rasoz was so close behind and there was no time to waste.

Jamar saw his wife surrounded in a golden dust ahead. He yelled out, "Get ready!" After he put Modie safely on the ground, Jamar ran towards Ashlar.

"Get ready for what, Dad?"

"Modie, we have no time for explanations." Reaching for his wife, he felt his body absorb and become one with the Royal Draugs. Together, hand in hand, Jamar and Ashlar stood in the meadow appearing like a golden illusion.

"What? What is going on?" Modie asked as he watched his parents slowly become invisible.

Ashlar spoke in a final voice, "Remember that all decisions come with consequences. We should have listened to your words, Modie. Now, we need to make amends. Your father and I are going to use my BellKey's power and The Royal Draugs to secure and protect the forest, containing Rasoz within. Yet again, we need you to complete the task given. You will need to go back into the forest and get your father's BellKey. Rasoz is a force to reckon with and could cause more destruction. Go to Flora, son. She will guide you. You have to do this alone now."

In shock, Modie watched his parents disintegrate completely into gold dust. Spinning and swirling their magic reached up in the sky only to part in two. Delicate golden bands went in opposite directions, spreading out circling their forest, and joining together again in front of Modie.

"*Alone?*" The word echoed in Modie's mind. "*I am all alone?*"

He stood in front of the golden veil wall that his parents made with the Royal Draugs and felt so very tired. Reaching his hand out, his brushed his fingers along the glittery substance.

"*Go, Modie! Go to Flora!*" His parents' thoughts entered his mind.

Modie shook his head and muttered, "No, no! I don't want to leave you! I don't want to be alone." Energy left the little Pilutar as exhaustion weighed him down. Allowing his body to collapse on the ground, Modie curled up next to the veil.

Rasoz, who was on the other side, saw the crumbled slight form. He charged forward and focused on Modie.

"HE IS MINE NOW!" Roaring Rasoz hit the golden wall only to be stopped. For standing at attention with shield drawn was a full-sized Royal Draug, with a fierce scowl on his face and his wings spanned out. Upon Rasoz's impact, the Royal Draug shoved his shield forward sending Rasoz flying back and landing with a bone-jarring thud. He was stunned; he sat up and shook his head.

Noir's cawing voice came from behind Rasoz.

"ATTACK!" Rasoz screamed.

Noir shot its feathered body like a missile straight into the Draug only to be sent soaring back next to Rasoz. Promptly, the Draug dissolved right back into the wall. Large, burnt black feathers floated in the air around the pair.

Rasoz blew a single feather from the front of his face and demanded, "Give me the BellKey, Noir. I will take care of this posthaste!" He held his hand out and looked at Noir. "Well?"

Shrugging his black wings up and down, Noir shook his beaked head.

"What do you mean you can't find it?" Rasoz bellowed as he stood up.

Noir began cawing and squawking, and Rasoz was getting fed up. He covered his ears in frustration. "I don't want to hear any more of your excuses! That BellKey is somewhere within this disgusting prison." Now pacing back and forth,

Rasoz reasoned. "And with all prisons there is always a way to escape." He stroked his chin with an eyebrow raised and contemplated. A movement on the other side of the wall caught his attention.

It was a small young buck, B.B., entering the meadow. B.B. saw his new friend, Modie, curled up in a ball, so he raced over.

"Modie, what is wrong?" B.B. asked as he nudged Modie with his nose.

When there was no response, B.B. looked around. It was then that he saw Rasoz with his evil smile. A moan from Modie brought B.B.'s attention back.

"B.B.?—very tired—all alone—need Flora." With that said, Modie fell back to sleep.

Determined now to help his friend, B.B.—with great effort—bent his small head down to try and scoop up Modie like his father did for him with his tiny antlers-to-be. He wanted to carry Modie to safety, away from the man with the ugly smile.

B.B.'s father entered the meadow in order to assist his son. Upon seeing Rasoz, the magnificent creature stomped its hoof, snorting in disgust. He tossed its regal head and went to Modie's curled-up body. He bent down on its forelegs and used his trophy antlers to scoop up the battle-worn figure.

"Thanks, Dad! He is all alone now and Modie said something about Flora."

"I am proud of you, B.B." Speaking to Modie, he said, *"Settle in, young Mighty Modie. I will carry you to your destination as I did for your father,"* the buck reassured the young warrior.

Half asleep, Modie adjusted himself onto the buck's back, nestling his face into the coarse fur. He smelled a familiar scent and mumbled, "Daddy?" Then he fell back into a dreamless sleep.

"That's right, you go to Flora whose power is so limited now. Run while you can because I WILL find your father's BellKey and the way to deal with you and your family," Rasoz vowed.

CHAPTER 14

The Golden Prison

After the school bell rang, children went safely home to do their homework and chores; unlike Maddie whose blue-jean clad legs skipped purposely across the bridge to the meadow towards Bellmaur Peak.

"I can't wait until I see Modie again! We can play in the forest and then I will bring him home with me. Then everyone will believe me that the BellKeepers are here!"

With her lucky ball cap firmly on her head and blonde curls bouncing with each step she took, Maddie entered the meadow. The sight of the glittery wall stopped her movement. Frowning with her head tilted to the side, Maddie slowly approached the swirling formation.

"This is so unbelievable!" She trailed her finger through the gold dust and felt a tickling travel up her arm.

"You are a beautiful child, Madeline."

Giggling, Maddie said, "Thank you! My granddad says I look like my ancestors, whatever that is. Hey, I can hear you in my head like with Modie! I am really getting good at this stuff." Maddie looked closely at the wall. "I am here to find proof of the BellKeepers. Do you know where Mighty Modie is?"

"Well, well! Things are looking up perfectly for us, Noir. We have a visitor, Modie's little friend. She would be the perfect bait to trap that meddlesome Pilutar. The question is how do we get her?"

Circling Rasoz's head, Noir cawed in a series of rapid, staccato sounds.

"Noir! Stop that cackling! I cannot think with all that noise . . . what?" Pausing, Rasoz finally listened to his feathered companion. A sudden sharp laugh of jubilation exploded from Rasoz's body. "You are brilliant, my feathered friend. Absolutely brilliant! If we can't go through the wall or around it, what is to stop us from going over it?" He took several steps back and raised his staff high above his head, whipping it in a fast circular motion. Round and round, the staff went forming into a blue whirlwind. The sound of thunder exploded as a tornado-like form reached up into the sky. With Noir leading the way, the configuration arched up and over heading straight for the unsuspecting Maddie.

"Run! Run, child, run!"

"Run? What do you mean run? Hey? Do you hear thunder? It isn't supposed to rain today. My mom would have made me take my umbrella if it were, you know."

Maddie searched the sky for any rain clouds and watched with horrified fascination. The large, black crow was coming right at her! Behind it was a storm cloud rolling forward. The haze took the form of a large hand with long fingers; talon-shaped fingernails curved towards her!

Screaming, Maddie ran back towards the bridge. She did

not make it far when she felt herself lifted up into the air, her lucky ball cap falling to the ground.

"Come, dear, it is time to wake up."

Modie felt a gentle hand shaking his shoulder, so he opened one eye. A little old lady smiled adoringly at him. Opening the other eye, he took in his surroundings. He was in Flora's cave! Flora, the Oracle!

He scrambled up from the feathered bed and addressed Flora by dropping to one knee, head bent down low.

"Precious child! Stand up! I am not your Oracle now. I am a good friend." Babbling away, Flora waved her arms around in excited gestures. "Such excitement you have had in just one day. Why, when my Royal Draugs told me what you could do, well, I was simply amazed! You know, we were not sure if anyone would be able to handle those BellKeys. But, you performed magnificently! The BellKeys have a great purpose, mind you. A powerful purpose, actually, but enough of that. You don't need to worry about that now." She looked down at Modie who was sitting on the floor, mouth wide open, red eyes dazed from just listening to what he thought was gibberish.

"Get up, dear boy! Get up! What are you doing on the floor? We have work to do so much work." She walked over to her stove and pulled out bell-shaped cookies that just finished baking. "I can't tell you how happy I am to finally have company. Always dreamed of having company. It never happened, but that is okay because I have had the perfect company all these years, ME!" Flora waved a cookie in the air to cool it off. "Cookie, dear?"

"Ah, no thank you." Standing, Modie alternately put his

hands behind his back, then in the front, unsure what he was supposed to do or say.

This was Flora, the Oracle of his people that his parents held so dear to their hearts. But, she looked like an old lady who was a little short in the mind department.

"Looks can be deceiving, Modie. I am surprised that you have not learned that by now," Flora calmly spoke.

Sheepishly, Modie nodded and mumbled an apology as they sat down.

"Enough of this. Come, share my cookies with me. Some are chocolate. You must love chocolate. I know that I do." Jumping up from the table Flora exclaimed, "Why, I have something for you, yes, I do! Something to put a smile on your face." Flora's rounded backside swayed as she went over to a large chest sitting on the floor.

With a grunt, Flora lifted the lid and started to rummage through all the items within. "Now, where is it? It has to be in here somewhere." Clothing and other articles flew up into the air as Flora tossed things one by one over her shoulder. "Ah, here it is! I just knew I would find it. Yes, I did. And would you look at this, I found it just like I thought, it is always in the last place you look. Of course, it is always in the last place you look, why would you keep looking if you have all ready found it? That would be ridiculous! Even if it is in the first place you look and you find it THEN it is the last place you look!"

Modie smiled and nodded his head and acted as if he followed and understood every word that Flora just spoke.

Coming back over to Modie, Flora placed a photograph of his parents—Ashlar and Jamar—before him. They were standing side by side with an arm wrapped around each other and smiling with such love. His father had one hand placed on his mother's stomach, which was well rounded in pregnancy.

"Thank you, Flora. You are right, this does bring a smile to my face." Modie said as he touched the picture of his parents. "But, how did you get this? You have been in this mountain for hundreds of years."

"Well, I am not without my sources, dear child! The Ancient Ones are in touch with me constantly. When I heard of who would be chosen as the BellKeepers, well, naturally I would like to see who they are. Of course, I was very fascinated about you! I even sent a special "gift" when you were born. Your talking to animals was from me."

"Really? No one knew how I got that one!"

"Just a little trick from the Oracle trade," Flora said with a secret smile.

Modie sat munching away on the bell-shaped treats wondering what he was supposed to do now.

"You need to go and get your father's BellKey, of course. After that everything will fall into place," said Flora, reading his mind yet again.

"How can I do that when my parents are gone?"

Reaching across the table, Flora held Modie's hand in hers. "Oh, Modie! They are not gone. Why, they are still inside you, inside your heart. After you get the BellKey all will be well, you will see." And with a reassuring pat on his hand, Flora stood.

"Okay, you will need more protection from that Rasoz. I really should have seen him coming but I have been limited in my sight. My magic is not very strong anymore, you know." In answer the golden walls flickered showing the hard, cold stone beneath. Flora continued, "Living here all this time has slowly diminished it. Thank the Tulips that my people have been protected within the Veil of Sanctuary. Now, where was I? Oh, yes, more protection."

Thinking out loud, Flora mumbled a bit to herself then loudly exclaimed, "Yes, you will need something fun, creative and filled with adventure. Oh, this is perfect, wonderfully perfect, you will have great fun with this! I know I did when I was a young girl and so perfect since Rasoz is the one who gave them to me in the first place." She clapped her hands in glee and smiled wide.

Then she closed her eyes and she raised her hands in the air. The bell around her neck rose forward, glowing bright as only an Oracle's could. A soft beacon of light came out of the bell, circling Flora's head. Several doors formed hovering in the air then spun within the wave of magic.

She threw her her arms out and the doors went skimming out of the cave settling within the forest below.

Out of breath, Flora sank into a chair. "Well, that took a lot out of me. Give me a minute, child, to regain my strength." Her Pilutar bell around her neck dimmed to a dull sheen. She picked up a cookie and nibbled on it. "Perfect energy food, this is," Flora uttered with her mouth full as she waved the cookie in the air.

She wiped her mouth with her sleeve and took a deep breath. "There! Much better. Now where were we? Goodness, I can't seem to keep up with everything."

"The doors?" Modie asked.

"Yes! Yes, your doors, dear Modie. They are your special playrooms. When you go on your journey to find your father's BellKey, they will be there for you!" She clapped her hands again. "So, what do you think?"

"About what?"

"The doors, silly boy!"

"What about the doors?"

"Modie, pay attention! The doors are your escape from Rasoz, didn't I tell you that?" Seeing Modie shake his head, Flora sighed. "Oh well, this is how the doors work. Whenever Rasoz is close by, your BellKey will ring. Now, mind you, it is not going to ring that pleasant twinkling sound you hear when your parents want you. Your bell will GONG," Flora yelled. "When you hear that gong, you go into the nearest door immediately. You will be safe there because Rasoz will NOT be able to go in after you, the Royal Draugs will see to that! Inside the door, dear, is where your true adventure will begin. The perfect place for you to play! I set up my absolute favorites for you. And when Rasoz is gone then your BellKey will ring that beautiful twinkling sound and you can leave your magical playroom and continue on your quest!"

Shooing Modie towards the exit of her home, Flora said, "Come on now! Time is wasting. Off you go! Find the Bell-Key." Modie, still a bit confused, reluctantly left. Flora called after his retreating back, "I will keep your picture safe for you, oh and remember the doors, dear!"

Upon entering the meadow, a small object lying on the ground caught Modie's attention. He walked slowly and kept his eyes on the item before him.

"Oh, no!" Modie recognized the ball cap that belonged to his new best friend, Maddie. He ran the rest of the way. Reaching down, he picked it up. Modie turned in a complete circle looking for his friend.

"Maddie!" he called but there was no answer.

"Rasoz has taken her, Son."

"Dad?" Going to the golden veil, Modie placed his hand

inside. Brighter the barrier burned, a feeling of warmth surrounded his hand. Pulling his hand back out, Modie asked, "But, how did he take Maddie and why?"

"That does not matter right now, son. Your friend is in the forest as we speak. She has been able to escape Rasoz's clutches but he is chasing her. You need to go inside and help her. NOW!"

Modie didn't waste any time. He put Maddie's lucky ball cap on top of his head and walked through the wall. Great pressure surrounded his body—making his back arch from the force. He stopped in the middle for a brief moment and allowed the presence of his parents to reach into his soul. Tiny gold particles flickered around him enveloping his entire body with love. Regret entered his mind for he knew that he could not stay.

"I will not fail you!" He promised as he took the final steps toward the prison of Rasoz.

GONG!

The loud clang startled Modie. It took him a brief moment to remember what that meant. Rasoz!

Then he heard a high-pitch wailing voice a short distance away. "Get away from me, you—you—well whatever you are!"

Modie heard Maddie's screams and running footsteps.

GONG! GONG!

Seeing one of the white doors with a gold knob that Flora made for him, Modie ran towards it.

He held the door knob with one hand and yelled for Maddie who was running near him.

"Maddie! Here, here! Come quickly!"

"Modie!" Curls flying Maddie's face broke into smiles as she raced towards her new friend. As she caught up to him she said, "Modie, am I glad I found you! Hey, you found my hat! And WOW, there is a door in the middle of the forest! Did you know that there is a man—"

GONG!

"I know! His name is Rasoz. He is the one destroying your forest." Modie opened the door hauling Maddie in after him.

Rasoz reached the door just as it closed behind the two pestering kids. Noir flew around in circles hovering above the portal.

"A Flora door, how typical!" Rasoz said as he reached for the golden doorknob. Upon contact, an electrical charge zapped his hand. He snatched his hand back and stepped back. "It is being protected, Noir!" He continued to walk all the way around the freestanding formation, checking it out from all angles. "I believe I am going to regret giving Flora this gift. It was a weak moment, Noir. But, in my defense, it was the only thing I could come up with to get her out of my hair. I was so busy plotting the downfall of the Kingdoms of Enchantment and that niece of mine was always underfoot. How ironic that she is now using those doors against me!"

Rasoz turned his back to the front of the door and casually walked away with Noir following. With a sudden movement, which had Noir cawing in surprise, Rasoz turned whipping out his staff, pointing it at the door. The blue beam shot out directly towards Flora's door. A Royal Draug's shield appeared completely covering the door. When the beam struck, it ricocheted back, striking Noir in his hindquarters causing more black feathers to float in the air.

Noir screeched and cawed his anger as he picked up his battered feathers from the ground.

Rasoz shrugged his shoulders in a dismal apology and said, "I believe Flora has outdone herself this time. However, time shall tell who will be the victor."

Spinning the crystal in front him, he concocted a plan in his mind. With a sinister smile he said, "We will just have to wait for them to come back out."

CHAPTER 15

Ranger Modie

As the door closed behind him, the first thing Modie noticed was the dry air that had a slight breeze. The second was a tumbleweed haphazardly stumbling down the middle of the dirt street where he was standing. Slow-moving rocking chairs creaked on the boarded walkway, while the old men who were lounging there smoked pipes and others spit their tobacco in the nearby spittoons. Horses were tied up to a post drinking water from a trough, others were leading wagons. A Bank, Butcher Shop, General Store were established on the right. Farther down on the left, Modie saw the Barber, Sheriff's Office and the Livery where horses were kept. Fancy-dressed ladies with parasols and bustled gowns smiled at Modie as they walked by, some even batting their eyelashes.

Suddenly a man's flying body crashed through a saloon window landing next to Modie's feet. Wiping off the dust that flew on his white western-cut shirt, Modie made a parting comment to the poor chap on the street as he made his way into the local saloon, "Cowboy, that window will cost ya a week's pay!"

Wow! Where did that twang come from? Modie thought.

"Yes, Ranger Modie, sir."

I am a Ranger!

Swaggering through the swinging saloon doors, Ranger Modie walked into the smoke-filled room, immediately taking in the surroundings. Music stopped and silence filled the air. Complete attention was on him, Ranger Modie.

Nothing unusual here, he noted. Just the typical cowboys and ranch hands that he knew well. Just some of the good ol' boys playing poker and shooting the bull.

There had been reports that the Barker Brothers were coming into town. They have robbed banks throughout the state but nobody touches Ranger Modie's town. With an ingrained caution, Modie continued in.

Clinking sounds came from Modie's spurs as he moseyed on up to the barkeeper.

"Howdy, Sam, give me the usual!" Ranger Modie said, slipping off his 10-gallon white cowboy hat and placing it next to him on the bar as he sat on the well-worn barstool.

"You got it!" Sam, the barkeeper, said as he finished wiping down a glass with his apron.

A foaming cup of hot chocolate slid down the bar.

Blowing off the top layer of whipped cream, Modie asked, as he downed his favorite beverage, "So, how's it been today?" Sam looked around and then leaned forward. "I heard some of them there men talkin'. Seems the Barker Brothers are plannin' on bein' in this here place high noon."

Ranger Modie reached into his pocket and pulled out a dollar bill, sliding it down the bar to Sam, the barkeeper.

"Ah, shucks, Ranger! Ya know yer money ain't good here." Sam said as he slid it back.

Placing his cowboy hat back on his head, he tipped it,

"Mighty obliged to you, Sam. You keep me informed, ya hear?"

Modie walked back through the saloon doors and stood on the boardwalk.

"This is so neat! We have to thank Flora for this door when we can!" Modie said out loud. "Now, where is Maddie?"

"MODIE!"

He glanced farther down in the middle of the street and saw a large feathered hat bobbing up and down. Attached to that was a face with an angry scowl. White lace and vivid red satin stormed forward.

"Hey, Ranger! That lil' woman of yers shur looks madder than a wet hen!" Raucous laughter followed one of the towns-people's comments.

Maddie blew a single, long blonde curl that had escaped her elaborate hairdo underneath the feathered hat and stood rather impatiently in front of Modie; a black buttoned-up boot tapping on the boardwalk.

"Well?" Maddie said, hands now on her hips.

"Howdy, Miss Maddie Mae."

A single lace-covered hand went up in the stop signal. "I have only one question fer you, *Ranger* Modie. It isn't the one 'bout how come we have been plucked down into this here ol' west town when we were just in a forest. It isn't the one about how come I can't stop talkin' like a country girl singer whose life has done gone bad. And it isn't even about why you are callin' me Miss Maddie Mae. Nope, it is just not one of those questions. What I really want to know is WHY AM I WEARIN' A FRILLY DRESS?" Maddie finished her tirade with her voice screeching as she plucked at a piece of the red satin skirt.

Sheepishly, Modie glanced at nearby townspeople with an embarrassed smile.

"Now, Maddie Mae, this is not the time to be a gettin' yer fine knickers in a knot. No, siree ma'am. Them Barker Brothers are a comin'. Why don't you find yerself a nice li'l ol' cubby hole to hide in while I play in this here adventure?"

"*Ranger* Modie, *darlin'*, don't you even think fer one cotton pickin' minute that I am goin' to stand by, twirlin' my thumbs, while you—"

Suddenly, there was an explosion into the air.

The force of the blast knocked Miss Maddie Mae right into Ranger Modie who, because he is such the fine gentleman, caught her with his strong arms and was able to stand her up on her own two feet without any trouble at all.

Townspeople fled into the street. One yelled at Ranger Modie, "The livery is on fire, Ranger!"

Immediately Ranger Modie went into action. "Sound the alarm for the volunteer firemen!" He ordered as he whistled for his horse. The clanging sound of the alarm echoed as Ranger Modie grabbed the reins of his Palomino. Swinging his body up into the saddle, he glanced down at Miss Maddie Mae.

"You stay right here. This won't take but a second." Nudging his horse forward, he galloped off, racing to the rescue of his beloved townspeople.

A fire brigade had formed with one man pumping water. The rest were in a single-file row passing filled buckets to each other. Once the water was dumped on the inferno, the bucket was passed once again to start the whole process. Soot covered faces and bodies milled around the nearby tables that the womenfolk had set up, laden with sandwiches and lemonade.

Everything was in order and working smoothly—the fire was in control; people were working together. But Ranger Modie still felt a prickle of uneasiness. Something was not quite right. Looking back towards the deserted town street, Ranger Modie noticed the two black stallions tied up near the Bank. The Barker Brothers were in town and Miss Maddie Mae was not where he left her!

"Deputy Doodle!" Ranger Modie hollered as he spied his so-called assistant sipping lemonade talking to Miss Sally Sue instead of helping the other workers. Nudging his horse forward, he approached the two.

He touched his hat's brim to acknowledge Miss Sally Sue, then turned his attention to his Deputy.

"Doodle, keep an eye out on these kind folks."

"Duh, shur Ranger, I can keep an eye on these folks. My other eye could then be on Miss Sally Sue." After hearing Miss Sally's giggle, Deputy Doodle grinned. "Where are ya goin' off ta?"

Ranger Modie urged his horse to a full trot and yelled back, "I have a bank withdrawal to make."

"Have you two no decency? Did your mama not teach ya any manners at all? You can't just come in here robbin' this here bank! These folks work darn hard for their dollar." Miss Maddie Mae's voice carried out the bank door to Ranger Modie's ears.

With a sigh, Ranger Modie tied up his horse next to the black stallions, "Nothin' can be simple. She just couldn't stay put. Nope, had to get herself tangled up with them there Barker Brothers. She is no doubt one brick short in the oven." Muttering to himself Ranger Modie approached the bank entrance. He took a quick peek in and saw Ernie the Teller with his arms high up in the air, standing behind the teller cage. Several bags filled to the brim with money were on the ground. The Barker Brothers were in front of the bags, but their attention was on Miss Maddie Mae who was still lecturing them.

Catching Teller Ernie's eye, Ranger Modie motioned with his hand to slowly get down. Then he settled himself right nicely against the door jamb, pulling his 10-gallon hat low down on his forehead, leaning there nonchalantly waiting to be noticed.

Tiny dust particles danced in the air as the afternoon sunlight cast Ranger Modie's shadow on the floor. He reached for his Colt 45 with the pearl-encrusted handle and drew the gun from its holster. Casually he clicked the chamber open checking on the number of bullets it contained. With a flick of the wrist the compartment closed, drawing the attention of the Barker Brothers away from Miss Maddie for a brief moment.

Bart Barker, the older of the two, immediately grabbed Miss Maddie Mae and wrapped a beefy arm around her neck, using her body as a shield.

When the other brother, Ralph Barker, saw Modie he drew his gun and pointed it directly at Ranger Modie.

"Well, well! Lookie here, Ralph. It is the legendary Ranger Modie." Bart said as he pulled his arm tighter around Miss Maddie Mae's throat. "And I heard him tell that this is your sweetheart. Ain't that cushy?"

"Modie? He has a gun, a rrreal gun!" Eyes wide and face white, Maddie lost all the bravado she had been feeling earlier.

"You just be quiet now, Miss Maddie Mae, I will take care of these here vermin'."

He put his gun back into its holster and took two steps in.

Ching, ching! The sound of his spurs echoed in the bank.

With feet braced wide, arms hung loose by his sides, Ranger Modie flexed his hands a few times before saying, "You have 'til the count of three to let go of this here lady."

"One."

"Whatcha goin' to do, Ranger? Huh? You have one gun pointed at cha. The other is on your sugar pie here."

"Two."

"We real scared, huh Bart?" replied Ralph.

A twinkling music came from Ranger Modie's bell underneath his cowboy shirt.

"Ah, man! Modie, we were just going to have a shoot out! It was just getting good, too!" Releasing Maddie, the man playing Bart Barker complained.

"What? What is going on? Aren't you going to shoot them? Modie! Do something now! And hey! What happened to my accent?" Stomping her foot Maddie yelled, "Will someone tell me what is going on?"

"Modie, did you not tell this young lady that this was all a game?" asked Ralph.

Coming from around the teller cage Ernie the Teller said, "Shame on you, Modie!"

"Are you telling me that none of this was real? That everyone was just pretending?" Maddie demanded.

"Wasn't it great, Maddie? Flora made these doors for me when I need to get away from Rasoz. There are even more in the forest!" He grabbed Maddie's hand and headed out the bank door. "It is safe for us to go back now so we need to hurry."

In the middle of the Old West Town, people, who participated in the playroom, were gathered. Maddie and Modie made their way through the crowd, getting pats on their backs and calls of good luck.

"Come back and play soon!" They all cried out to the two.

As the crowd parted, Ernie glanced at the man who played Bart. "You were really good! I really believed your character."

Bart replied, "You know, there *was* a moment when I truly was one with the bank robber. You were good, too."

Seeing the white door at the edge of the town, Modie strode purposely towards it. Maddie followed close behind, wobbling some in her button-up boots.

"Hurry up, Maddie. We need to get my father's BellKey."

"You know, Modie, this was not part of any stories my granddad told me. He never mentioned once about Flora making doors to play in."

"Maddie, we have to get back into the forest while it is safe. Rasoz is not around, so hopefully we can make it back to the mountain and get my father's BellKey." Modie reached for the gold knob and turned.

"Listen, Modie! Are there going to be any more doors? You have to prepare me before we go through them. I mean, I like surprises and all but the frilly dress stuff is just too much, you know. Maybe you can pick something more casual."

With a sly grin, Modie shot a look at his friend. Then without a word proceeded to open the door.

"What does *that* look mean? And have I done enough to get a BellKey yet?" Maddie's voice faded as they walked through the door to the waiting forest.

CHAPTER 16

Dylan, Jake and Joelle

W e will find her, Dylan." Jake reassured his best friend.
Dylan looked over at Jake who was still wearing his practice football jersey. Jake, who is the star quarterback for the LaHiere Junior High School, stood a few inches taller than Dylan and is twice his size. His black hair was still slicked with sweat from his team's workout.

"Yeah, thanks for cutting your practice short for me. Did Coach Jennings mind?"

"Nah, all I had to do was mention Maddie's name. You know how everyone in the town likes that kid."

"I should have known that she was going to take off after school. When I came home and saw the scribbled note about getting the proof on the BellKeepers, I panicked."

Seeing the bridge ahead Jake said, "Well, more than likely she is over there in the meadow and we will be back before your parents even know that she was gone."

"Hey, you two wait for me!" A girl's voice called from behind them.

Dylan turned around and saw Joelle, Jake's twin sister in her cheerleader uniform, running towards them. Her long black hair, pulled back in a ponytail, was swinging back and forth from her running.

"Oh great," muttered Dylan whose heart just kicked in double-time.

"What are you doing here? Why aren't you at cheerleading practice?" demanded Jake in a rude tone.

Joelle's green eyes flashed with indignation. "I am not stupid, Jake, something is wrong! I was on the field practicing when I saw Dylan pull you out of your work-ups. And since nothing short of death would take you away from your precious football team, I knew it was serious. So, what is going on?" Jake turned the question on to Dylan, who was just standing there staring at Joelle.

"Dylan?" Joelle asked again.

"Huh? Oh! Ummm, Maddie went looking for proof of the BellKeepers. We were on our way to the forest to find her."

"Okay, count me in."

"You are going with us? As in—here—with me?" Dylan practically squeaked.

"Yes, with you and my brother." Starting to feel impatient, Joelle put her hands on her uniformed hips. "Do you have a problem with that?"

"Ummm no, no problem. Do you have a problem with it, Jake?"

Jake forced himself not to smile at the look of panic on Dylan's face. He knew his friend liked his sister and had problems communicating with her, let alone being in the same vicinity. "It will probably help having an extra pair of eyes."

"Great, just great." Muttering to himself, Dylan starting walking across the bridge. The other two fell into step beside him. Sarcastically, he whispered towards Jake, "Thanks for the help."

"What?" Joelle asked.

"Ummm, I said thanks for the help," Dylan gave a telling look over at his now ex-best friend.

Jake reached over his petite sister's head, who was walking in between them, and cuffed his best friend's shoulder. "Glad to be of service, Dylan. We always seem to pull Maddie out of one mess or another."

Joelle laughed, remembering a time from the past. "Oh yeah! Remember when Maddie decided the water tower was too gray and ugly?"

The two boys groaned in unison.

"You two found her just when she had finished painting bright pink tulips all over the tower. By the time you helped her get the paint down that she "took" from Mr. Winter's Hardware dumpster, you guys were covered in pink paint and of course, Maddie looked clean as a whistle. You two had to repaint the whole tower plus several Main Street storefronts that summer as punishment."

"Hey! Maddie didn't have the lid on tight and it was hard getting up and down those stairs," Jake protested.

"She never did say how she got all that paint up there in the first place," mused Dylan. "Besides, that was granddad's fault for telling her all those fairy tales. She goes off into la-la land whenever he talks about the Pilutars. Then the next thing we know she does a crazy stunt. Just like now! Yesterday she came home and in the middle of her party she kept going on and on about BellKeepers and having proof. I just hope she is around this forest somewhere. I am starting to get a little worried."

"My point was that you guys always cover for Maddie."

"I am not covering for her this time. I just want to find her." Dylan responded with an edge of uneasiness in his voice.

As they climbed the hill that was before the meadow, he

continued, "Maddie has always been weird about granddad's stories. She believes in the Pilutars and the BellKeepers. Personally, I think it is all a fairy tale. Just a story that granddad made up."

"Uh, Dylan? Are you sure it is just a story?" Joelle asked with a hitch in her voice.

Looking up, wondering why Joelle sounded funny, Dylan saw that she made it to the meadow before he and Jake did. "Yeah, I'm sure!" he said.

Scrambling the rest of the way, they were almost to the top when Dylan asked her, "Why? Don't tell me that you believe in it?"

"I didn't until now."

"What?" Jake and Dylan said in surprise.

"Look!" Joelle said as she pointed to the forest.

The two boys turned their gazes to where Joelle indicated. There at the edge of the meadow was a golden wall, shimmering in the afternoon sunlight.

"This does not look good," Jake said.

"Please, please someone tell me that my sister is not in there!"

The three teenagers walked slowly towards the magical vision. Each reached the same conclusion.

"Knowing Maddie, Dylan, she is in there." Joelle looked closely around. "It appears that this, whatever it is, stretches all the way around the forest. But, I can't really tell from here."

Jake came over to stand next to Dylan, speaking in a hushed tone. "Why don't you and Joelle go up the mountain and get a better view. I can stay down here in case Maddie shows up."

"You want me to go up that mountain with Joelle? Alone?"

"She is just my sister. You were just talking to her a minute ago with no problem."

"That was different! You are here. I can't put two words together if I am by myself with her and you know it!"

"What are you two whispering about?" asked Joelle.

"Just trying to figure out what to do. Why don't you and Dylan go up the mountain and check things out. I am going to stay here in the meadow. Check out this gold thing here. Maybe there is a way around it."

"Great idea, Jake! Come on Dylan." He grabbed hold of Dylan's hand and pulled him towards the mountain. "There is a cliff edge just a short distance up. We can check things out from there."

Hoping he wouldn't embarrass himself by saying or doing something stupid, Dylan allowed himself to be led to the mountain. Of course, once he realized that he, Dylan Hemis, class president of LaHiere Junior High, the biggest bookworm of the school, was holding Joelle Campbell's hand—the girl of his dreams—his heart plummeted causing him to stumble on some loose rocks and landing face first on the ground.

"My humiliation is complete," he mumbled.

"Are you okay?" Holding her hand out again to help him up, Joelle was wondering what Dylan's problem was.

Dylan ignored her hand and figured it was best that he did not touch her. He scrambled back up. "Yeah, I am fine. Just lost my footing some," he said as he brushed off his now dirty polo shirt and jeans.

"Will you two hurry up?" yelled Jake.

"Sometimes I wonder why he is my best friend!" Dylan muttered to himself.

"Are you talking to yourself again?" questioned Joelle as she continued on up the mountain face.

Sighing, Dylan followed, thinking of the revenge he would enact upon Jake and his sister, Maddie, who if it was not for them, he would not be here with Joelle in the first place.

Jake watched their progress before turning his attention to the golden wall. Vaguely he could see the forest through it.

Wondering if it was possible, Jake picked up a small stone and threw it at the wall. Immediately a hole opened and the rock passed through. For a brief moment Jake was able to see the forest clearly.

"FAN—TAS—TIC!"

Jake paced back and forth and reasoned out loud. "If that rock could go through, then one should be able to think that I could go through." He stopped and took another look at the wall. "Okay, you can do this, Jake. You know you can. Just look at it like it is the opposing football team. YEAH! That is it!"

Pacing once again, Jake pumped himself up. He imagined hearing the crowd's yells and cheers. "You are on the 2 yard line, 15 seconds to go in the 4th quarter. Your team is down by 5. You need a touchdown to win the game. Call is made as a quarterback sneak." Panting out short staccato breaths, Jake went into formation.

He faced the wall and crouched down with his hands cupped in front of him. Then he checked out his "line" from side to side and started the quarterback cadence, "Blue 46; Blue 46; Hut, Hut!" Jake yelled in a booming voice.

The invisible ball was hiked into his hands. He tucked it into his arm and charged forward issuing a battle cry as he propelled his body towards the golden wall. A large hole opened allowing Jake access, who ended his rush through the opposing football team's line, winning the game. He threw the fake ball to the ground and did his team's victory football dance in the end zone.

"Whoa! Whoa! YES! I did it!" With arms raised high in the air and fists closed, Jake danced around in circles.

"Jake, Jake! I'm in here, Jake!"

Jake stopped dancing as soon as he heard his name called. "Maddie? Is that you?" Turning around, he saw a door with a black knob free standing behind him. It was slightly opened.

"*Hurry, Jake, hurry!*" The distorted voice called again.

"Maddie?" Hesitantly, Jake approached the door. His hand reached out and encountered the knob pushing the door open farther.

A rustling sound from behind him had Jake whirling around. Cawing and screeching filled his ears. Black, winged feathers slapped him in the face. He threw his arms up to ward off the attack and put himself off balance and fell backwards into the opened door.

Swiftly coming around from the back of the door, Rasoz grabbed the knob and pulled the door shut.

"One meddlesome teenager down; two more to go. Not to mention our dear friend Mighty Modie and Maddie, too!" Rasoz glanced up towards the mountain and noted Dylan and Joelle's progress. "Those two will have to wait. We must focus on the two who went through the Pilutar door. Flora thinks she is so smart but she forgets that I designed those doors for her."

With a wave of his staff, more doors appeared practically identical to Flora's that she had made for Modie. Another wave had them scattering throughout the forest.

"Let us just see what happens when they go through one of my doors like that wannabe football player did." With an evil laugh, Rasoz headed towards the entrance to the caves within the mountain, yelling out instructions to Noir.

"Watch for them to exit. They have to come out of that playroom door sooner or later. I will be waiting inside."

CHAPTER 17

'Tis Me Treasure

H ey, you still have on my lucky ball cap!" Maddie exclaimed. She reached over and snatched it off Modie's head as he was closing the playroom door and settled it over her blonde curls.

Modie rubbed the top of his head with a frown on his face and looked at the dead forest before them. Sighing, he realized the area was still in the same sadden state. The Old West playroom was nice for a while but he felt the pressure of everything he must accomplish and accomplish he must and soon!

"Why are you rubbing your head?" Maddie asked.

"I don't know. It hurts some."

"Did I hurt you when I took off the ball cap?" Standing on tiptoe, Maddie perused the top of Modie's head. "You aren't bleeding. Maybe you hurt yourself in the playroom though I don't remember you falling or anything. Do you have a headache? My mom takes medicine if she has a headache. I don't know if Pilutars can have medicine. So, do you have a headache?"

"No, but one can start any minute now."

"Hmmm, okay. Are you sure?"

"Maddie, I am fine. The top of my head hurts some. Maybe it was from wearing that huge cowboy hat." Modie said as he waved Maddie away from him. He walked over to a lifeless tree, sat down and rested his head back. He closed his eyes and wished that everything were normal again, whatever that means.

"Are you sure you are okay?" Maddie questioned yet again as she sat next to Modie. "You can have my lucky ball cap back if you are not."

Smiling now Modie said, "Thanks Maddie, but I am fine. Probably just a bit tired."

A scraping sound above them brought their eyes to the main trunk of the tree they were leaning on. Noir sat there calmly, looking down at them with what appeared to be a smile on his pointed beak.

"Soon, Mighty Modie, soon. We will have everything we wanted. Why don't you give up now and accept it. You are so tired and worn out. Time to let it go. It was so unfair of your parents to put so much on you. You were bound to fail from the beginning."

"Stop! Stop talking to me!" Modie yelled as he jumped up.

"What? I haven't said a word in at least two minutes, you know!" Maddie replied, standing next to Modie.

"Not you! That black bird, Noir."

GONG!

"Rasoz is near. We have to find another door." Looking around, Modie spied one behind the tree. He grabbed Maddie's hand and said, "Come on! We need to go through that one over there."

GONG! GONG!

He led Maddie to the solitary white door and thought it

would just be so nice to have a nap. He turned the gold door knob and pushed the door open. "Oh, Maddie? Be prepared!"

"Huh?" she grunted before she was pulled into the doorway that Modie had chosen.

Brilliant colors streaked by their faces as a black void opened before them. Losing Maddie's grip panicked Modie for a brief moment but the smell of salty air and water lapping against a solid force soothed his senses.

Modie closed his eyes. And lying down on the black surface, he decided that a wee bit o' nap was in order.

"Cap'n, Cap'n."

Feeling his shoulder shake, Modie the Red, opened his eyes immediately leaping from his bunk, drawing his cutlass from the sheath on his side, ready to do battle. He glanced around his quarters and saw that everything was in order and tightly secured to the bulkhead.

"Cap'n, 'tis me, Squid, ya Cabin Boy." Hands out attempting to ward off any attack, Squid warily watched his Captain come fully awake.

Modie the Red put his faithful cutlass back in place, and rubbed a hand over his face. "Squid, me boy! Have I not told ya, never wake me up 'tis way. You mustn't put the fear in me soul. Ya never know what I would do to ya."

"Sorry, Cap'n."

"Never ya mind. What 'tis so blastin' important that I couldn't have a wee bit o' shut eye?"

"I needs ya topside, Cap'n. The men are threatin' mutiny, they are. That prisoner of yers is causin' a bit o' ruckus, if ye don't mind me sayin' so."

"How can a wee slip o' girlie cause problems fer me men?"

"Well, ya see now, there's a feelin' that this here ship 'tis jinxed now. Ya know how sailors are superstitious 'bout womenfolk onboard. She be also sittin' on top of the bounty. Say she, 'tis her treasure and no canna touch it."

Sighing, Modie the Red adjusted his red kerchief with the white polka dots on his head. He checked the slings across his chest that held his four loaded flintlocks and made his way to the door leading to the passageway.

"Canna be too bad, Squid. What harm could a lassie truly do?" With that said, Modie the Red exited his chambers with Squid following closely behind.

Obviously, she could do a lot of damage. Modie the Red's crew, normally in order, was in complete confusion. Two of his men had their hands around each other's throats. Another pair was in a sword fight. Three were circled around the bounty with a young girl sitting primly on top of it.

"'Tis your cutlass," the lass said pointing to one pirate. "'Tis your pistol, 'tis your flintlock," she said to each in turn. Patting the treasure chest that was spilling its contents on the ship's deck, "'Tis me treasure!" she finalized with a smug smile upon her face.

Modie the Red knew that there was not much time to waste before his men were completely unmanageable. He turned and climbed several steps that took him to the quarter-deck giving him the advantage of seeing his crew below him.

Seeing one man with his hands around the ship's wheel guiding his darlin' through the waters, Modie the Red acknowledged him with a nod, "I will be takin' over the helm shortly, Sam."

"You got it, Cap'n."

Modie the Red raised his flintlock high into the air and fired off a single shot, which established complete silence from his men except for the young girl sitting on his bounty of treasure.

"Modie! Modie! I'm so glad to see ya. Lookie what I have here. Do we get to keep it? Such fine things!" Maddie said as she leaped up and opened the treasure chest, pulling out strands of pearls and placing them over her head. She promptly stuffed coins and gold pieces into the pockets of her cotton day dress with its high-neck lace collar.

She looked up at her best friend and continued, "Seeing all this here treasure keeps me mind off the fact that yet again I am talkin' funny. Why this time I sound like a wee leprechaun. And need I remind you that I'm a wearin' a frilly dress, I am. Not too mention, mind ya, that this here collar is choking me throat. Can't you come up with different costumes? So, me question is now, Do we get to keep this here treasure? We do, don't we?"

With that comment the three pirates, who were facing off with her, drew their weapons and pointed them directly at the prisoner intending to do bodily harm.

"Halt!" commanded Modie the Red. His men, who out of respect, immediately backed down.

"Lady Madeline," he addressed the young girl. "May I remind you that you are MY prisoner. You are not allowed the liberties you have a taken. I am Cap'n Modie the Red, legend to these here uncharted waters. This is my ship *Bells Toll*, greatly feared by all. We plundered your ship and took that there treasure. It was unfortunate that you were onboard but as a rule we do not harm womenfolk. That rule can be changed very fast, indeed."

"Modie the Red, Modie the Red!" Chanted his crew of

pirates, cheering that their Cap'n was siding with them instead of the lassie.

Lady Madeline continued rummaging through the bountiful chest and just waved off Modie, completely ignoring him. She gave a squeal of delight as she pulled an item from the chest.

"You brought me lucky cap!" Putting her ball cap on her head, she grinned at Modie the Red whose face was getting as red as his eyes.

"Do you think that this is all a game?" he roared.

"Sure, isn't it? Modie? This is a playroom isn't it? You said in the forest that this here was a playroom. Be prepared, ya said. Aye, that ya did." Doubt started to enter Lady Madeline's mind as she watched Modie the Red pace back and forth on the quarter-deck. Her eyes grew wide when he stopped and drew his large cutlass out and held it up in the air.

Modie the Red faced his men and yelled, "Tie her up! She walks the plank!"

A gigantic roar filled the sky from his men as they hustled to do his bidding.

Around and around the rope went, binding Lady Madeline.

As she was led to the plank that extended out over the sea, she called out to Modie the Red. "I really do not see the fun of this. Walk the plank! Ha! 'Tis such a joke."

She was pushed and prodded until she was standing on the small platform. "Okay, okay, I'm here and on the plank. But, this is really goin' too far now, ya know."

"Ahoy Cap'n." The call came from high above.

Modie the Red looked up to the crow's nest where his watchman was guarding the ship. His job was to look out across the sea for any enemy ships that may be passing by.

"Aye, Sigs. What do ya have for me?"

"'Tis a ship at 2 o'clock, mind ye. Full sail at us, she is. I canna rightly make out her flags."

"Hold tight, Sigs. I'm on me way. Keep her in ya sights, man."

Sheathing his cutlass, Modie the Red grabbed the hand railing on either side that led to the main deck. With his feet straightforward and out, he propelled himself down by sliding on the rails. As his feet hit the deck, his men parted to allow him room. Immediately Modie the Red navigated the shroud, a web of rope, to the main mast. He wrapped his body around the mast and shimmied up and into the crow's nest.

"Gimme your spyglass, Sigs." Pulling the telescopic piece out, he brought it to his eye and searched the area for the ship in question.

"MODIE!" A female voice yelled. "There is water below me here! Does Flora know that I canna swim? You do know that, don't ya. I will sink fer sure and never come up again." As Lady Madeline's balance started to wobble, she yelled up to the Captain, "Can you, *please*, stop this boat from a rockin'?"

"Blast it, girlie! I am conducting business here! And 'tis not a boat but a ship. And she will rock when she wants ta." Turning his attention back to the matter at hand, Modie the Red saw the galleon heading his way.

Handing Sigs back his spyglass, Modie the Red said in a firm voice, "Sigs, that is Her Royal Majesty's Navy, fer sure. Haul down the Jolly Roger flag. They will be a knowin' we are a pirate ship if they see the skull and cross bones on this here black flag. Hoist the British flag in 'tis place. We may cause a bit o' confusion then."

"Aye, aye, Cap'n."

As Sigs went about his work, Modie addressed his crew.

"Men, the Royal Navy is approaching us. We need ta be on guard now. It wouldna surprise me a bit that they are looking fer that lassie on that there plank. She needs ta jump to Davie Jones Locker and she needs to go now!"

At his command several of the pirates drew their weapons and approached the plank that had the standing Lady Madeline all trussed up on it.

"If ye think I am goin' ta jump in this here water, ya have another thing comin' ta ya! I told ya I can no swim, Modie. Are ya listenin' to me now? I CANNA SWIM! And by getting all wet it will be the death of me now. You are gonna save me, aren't you Modie?"

"You are so right, Lady Madeline! Cannot have that now can we?"

Drawing his cutlass once again, Modie the Red put it between his teeth. He leaped up to the rim of the crow's nest and grabbed a line from the main mast. Then he jumped into the air and used the rope to swing down to the waiting Lady Madeline.

"I'm so happy ya see me reasoning now, Modie. I am ready to leave this here playroom of yers." Smiling, the Lady Madeline watched Modie the Red's flight towards her.

Instead of feelin' her body snatched up into Modie the Red's arms and takin' her to safety, she felt her lucky ball cap plucked from her head. Astonished, she watched him put that cap on his own head. Taking the cutlass from his mouth he cut the line, stopping his flight where he landed perfectly back on the main deck in front of his crew.

"We canna be having this cap get wet now can we, lassie?" Grinning, Modie the Red turned his back to Lady Madeline's shrieks of anger.

He then went back up to the quarter-deck and told his man

Sam that he would take over the helm. As he approached the ship's wheel, Modie the Red turned the lucky ball cap backwards so that the bill rested on his neck.

A cannon shot echoed in the salty air. The black ball shot across the forecastle deck.

"We have a fight on our hands, maties!" Modie the Red yelled as he grabbed hold of the ship's wheel. "Man yer weapons, hold steady now!" With a sharp turn of the wheel the *Bells Toll* came about to the right. Belatedly, Modie the Red remembered the angered lassie.

He glanced at the plank and saw Lady Madeline fall to her buttocks and then come sliding back towards the main deck, shrieking words that would do his pirates proud.

"Aye, we may make her a sailor yet!" he said.

A beautiful twinkling sound entered the air calling a stop to the fun and games.

"Not again, Modie!" The entire pirate crew of the *Bells Toll* threw their weapons on to the ship's deck in frustration.

"Sorry, guys. But the forest is clear now. I really must go."

The solitary door appeared on deck beckoning Modie.

"Come on Maddie. We have to go now," Modie said as he walked towards the waiting entrance.

"*Excuse me?* We have to go now? Why do you get to call the shots? You said this wasn't a game. You had me on a gangplank Modie! There was water below me! I can't swim. I told you that. And I am sitting here, still tied up and in a frilly dress. This was not a playroom. It was a nightmare. And when are you going to untie me? Let me tell you something! I get to pick the next door. Do you hear me Modie?"

"Maddie," sighed Modie. "Just move your arms and you will be free. That is all you have to do."

Maddie wiggled her body and felt the ties unravel. As she

hustled to stand, the ropes pooled at her feet. "Fine! I still get to pick the next door."

Now walking side by side they approached the white door.

Maddie stopped Modie from opening the door with her hand on his arm. "You went right by me, Modie. You saved that hat." Gesturing to the ball cap still on Modie's head, "Instead of me. You were going to save me, right?"

Modie shot a look at his friend.

"There's that look again! Why do you do that instead of answering me?"

CHAPTER 18

Hocus Pocus

I don't see Jake. Do you?" Standing on the cliff that overlooked the entire village and forest, Joelle asked Dylan who was by her side.

"No, but he probably is walking around that gold ring. Look at it! It really does circle the forest."

"I am getting a funny feeling about this, Dylan. There is more to all of this than what we are seeing and I bet your sister is in the middle of whatever is happening. We have to find a way into the forest."

Dylan kicked a rock off the cliff in frustration and responded in a sharper tone than he intended. "Yeah, I know. But, how in the world can we get into that area? We don't even know what that gold stuff is. If we can't get in and Maddie is in there, does that mean that she is trapped?" Running his hands through his hair in anger, Dylan felt defeated. "UGH! This is too much! We are going to need help."

A mouthwatering aroma teased their nostrils. It was such a sweet smell that made them a bit dizzy. Reaching out for Joelle's arm, Dylan pulled her away from the cliff's edge.

"Do you smell that?" he asked.

"Where is it coming from?"

Looking at the mountain wall in front of them, Dylan pointed to it. "It seems to be coming from there. But, that would be impossible."

"*Nothing is impossible, child. You just have to believe,*" a feminine voice replied.

"Who was that?" Joelle asked Dylan who was not listening because he had already approached the rocky formation.

"Joelle, there is someone behind here!"

Beautiful twinkling music sounded causing Dylan to step back to Joelle. Together they watched in horror as a ray of light seeped through the mountain towards them. Gradually, the brilliant beam formed into an encompassing eight-foot diameter circle, cutting a hole from within the mountain out. Yellow stones that gleamed in the afternoon sunlight forged in rapid succession establishing a magical barrier. The formation swirled like a mist.

Dylan cautiously walked up and brought his focus closer to the mountain face. There, right before him, were miniature creatures all in gold marching back and forth.

"Joelle! There are tiny men! You have got to see this!" Dylan motioned to Joelle to come over. When Joelle was near, Dylan grabbed her hand and pulled her closer. "Just look at this!" Dylan put a single fingertip against the wall in hopes of making one of the gold creatures to halt.

Upon seeing its forward movement blocked, one of the Royal Draugs briefly stopped and looked over at the two mortals staring so intently at him and the others. With mocking stare back and a shrug of the shoulders, the Draug continued forward, walking through Dylan's finger causing both Joelle and Dylan to gasp. Frozen in shock, Dylan stood there with

Draug's following in single file through his finger. Joelle grabbed Dylan's hand and jerked it away from the mountain.

"Oh my gosh! That was unbelievable! They went right— they went right—," stuttering Joelle tried to finish her thought.

Dylan immediately stepped in front of Joelle, blocking her view of the little gold men. "I know. You don't need to say a word. As a matter of fact, I think we should just keep this to ourselves. No one would believe us anyhow," Dylan said as he shook his hand and double checked to make sure that some of those things were not crawling all over him.

The golden wall behind Dylan glowed and pulsed. He glanced over his shoulder and watched a few of the little men fly around.

"Now what?" Turning swiftly which caused some of his hair to fall out of place, Dylan took Joelle's hand and together they watched as the tiny creatures flew around like fireflies. Some skimmed over Dylan's hair, where he could sworn that he felt them smoothing his gel-slick hair back in place. Joelle swatted at them while Dylan ducked.

"Dylan! Make them stop!"

A soft twinkling music whispered through the mountain, yet again. Immediately, the Royal Draugs responded by flying in two directions and forming golden pillars on either side of the circle. As more Draugs left the circle, a hole formed where Dylan and Joelle could see inside. A living area could barely be seen with a shadowed figure pacing in the background. Once again, music filled the air and the golden pillars made up of the tiny men on each side of the entrance became a single Royal Draug in full size marking the entrance. Both were in full battle armor and a blank expression on their scrunched-up bulldog faces.

"What are we suppose to do now?" Joelle whispered to Dylan.

"I am assuming that we are to go in."

After making sure he firmly had Joelle's hand in his, Dylan took a step forward. Swiftly, the Royal Draugs brought their shields out blocking the teenagers' path.

"Okay, maybe not," said Dylan before taking a step back.

"Dylan, there is an old lady in there. You can see her moving."

More music sounded with a voice calling out an order.

"Stand down, boys. Dylan and Joelle are our friends. Welcome, welcome! Oh, how I so love company," the feminine voice said.

"She knows our names! How does she know our names?" Joelle said in a panicked voice.

Quickly moving in front of Joelle, Dylan looked over his shoulder and said, "Don't be scared. I will protect you, Joelle. Stay back and let me handle this."

"Scared? Me? Of what?" Joelle asked with false bravado even though she still clutched Dylan's arm.

Seeing the occupant inside the entrance, Joelle's body immediately relaxed. "Protect me from what? Handle what? Her?" Joelle pointed over Dylan's shoulder to the little old lady. "She looks like everyone's grandmother," she continued as she let go of his arm. But then noticing the antennae she mumbled, "Except for the things on her head."

"Sure, Joelle. Whatever you say!" Seeing the old woman wink at him, Dylan laughed.

Joelle stepped around her supposed protector and promptly approached the old woman who was busily munching on a cookie. "Okay! Who are you and what have you done to Maddie?"

"By the Tulips, child! You are a forward one, aren't you?

Of course, you always were growing up. Come in, come in! You too, Dylan," she called to the young man who was still standing outside staring at the golden men.

Dylan walked slowly inside the cave noting the golden walls that flickered every now and then. The rest of the cave held a warm, welcoming atmosphere that instantly put him at ease. Seeing Joelle looking at him with her hands on her hips caused him to ask, "What? This is really fascinating! Those flying things became a single person or whatever it is!"

"Yes, well, those are the Royal Draugs, my protectors. Now, come forward and have a seat." Flora motioned to her table, "Have some of my bell cookies. Quite delicious if I do say so myself. Oh! Did you hear that? I just did say so. Actually, please do ask myself and she would be happy to tell you how delicious they are. Me, myself and I fight over these cookies everyday. I usually win, of course. I'm sure if you asked me or myself they would say that they win." Laughing, the old woman sat and in a hushed tone she whispered, "I let them win sometimes, after all I do have to maintain my girlish figure."

"Who are you?" Dylan and Joelle, completely confused, asked in unison as they sat at the table. "Goodness, did I not say? Why I am, Flora. Once Oracle to the Pilutars."

"*You* are Flora? Then it really all is true, isn't it?" Joelle said as she put her elbows on the table leaning forward, "Then Maddie was right! Did you hear, Dylan? This is Flora! If anyone would know where Maddie is, it would be her."

"Do you, Flora? Do you know where my sister is?"

"Exactly? No. Is she safe?" She shrugged her shoulders and continued. "For now she is. She is with Modie and they are having a grand adventure. As long as they stay away from Rasoz and find Jamar's BellKey, all will be wonderful soon."

"I'm sorry, Flora, but I am not following you," Dylan said.

"Yeah, I'm not either," Joelle echoed.

"By the Tulips, did I not tell you? Goodness where is my mind today?" The golden walls dimmed once again startling Dylan and Joelle.

Red-faced in embarrassment, Flora excused herself from the table. With her head slightly down, she approached the wall that had flashed on and off. "I know, I know! My reserves are low. But, do you have to remind me when I have company? This is very humiliating," she admonished the mysterious wall in a hushed tone.

"Joelle, is she *talking* to that wall?" Dylan asked in a stage whisper as he leaned close to her.

From the side of her mouth she answered in kind, "Ohhh Dylan, it is worse than that! I think *the walls are answering her!* Shhh! She is coming back!"

Smoothing her hair way from her face, Flora took a deep breath as she came back to the table and joined the two teenagers. "I do apologize for that interruption. *Some* can be very pushy in reminding me that my magic is almost depleted. Such a crime to get old. Now, where was I? Oh! Yes, Modie and the BellKeys. I am sure you know the Legend of Bell-Keepers."

"How could we not? That story is the only thing my grand-dad tells Maddie who just lives for hearing it." Dylan frowned. "But, what does that have to do with my sister missing?"

"Hey! Didn't she mention this Modie's name to us? I could swear that she did. You know, during her party?" Joelle offered, her eyes bright with excitement.

"You are right! She did mention that name when she came back home. Flora, who is this Modie and where can we find him?" Dylan anxiously asked.

"Children, children! There is so much more that you need

to know before taking off to find Maddie. Now, listen to me and I will bring you up to date."

Flora told the unbelievable story of Rasoz and how she called in the BellKeepers to help. She explained about Modie and the tragedy that forced his parents to contain the forest.

"You mean that gold dust we saw surrounding the forest is *actually* Modie's parents? Joelle asked.

"And my sister is somewhere in there with Modie trying to get the third BellKey so that this Rasoz guy can be stopped?"

"Exactly! Well, except that there are Royal Draugs helping them, too. But, that is something else entirely." Flora continued, "What are you waiting for? Time is wasting! Your help is needed. Stand together right over there." She pointed to the area in front of her and rubbed her hands together then clapped them with glee. "Yes! I will just pouf you inside the forest and you can help."

"Pouf? What do you mean pouf?" Dylan's voice squeaked in shock.

Joelle, who's standing next to Dylan, agreed. "I don't want any hocus-pocus done on me!"

"Oh, be still my bell! Hocus-pocus, indeed! Why, I have never done anything of that sort. Hold hands now and stand still, mind you." In a cautious tone Flora continued, "Whatever you do don't move a muscle. This should not hurt a bit." The walls flickered when they heard her comment.

Quickly Flora turned and snapped a response, "That was an isolated incident as you well know!"

The walls flickered, yet again.

"I know I failed that class. I just could not get the whole disappearing thing. Fine! Fine! Have it your way!" Flora turned back to the teenagers.

"Okay, so where were we? Oh, yes that's right! Don't

move. Well, you can breathe, of course. Just don't move. It will only take a second."

Holding her bell in one hand, Flora waved her arm towards the young teenagers and yelled, "Hocus-pocus!"

She laughed at herself and the teenagers' expressions, "Oh, that was just a joke," Flora said. "I am so funny. My, but I love my sense of humor. Get ready now and here we go!" With a final wave of her arm, a door appeared directly behind Dylan and Joelle.

"There you go. Walk through here," Flora said as she opened the door. "It will take you two straight into the forest."

As they walked through with a doubtful look, Flora called out one more time, "Watch out for the doors!"

Her golden walls faded again as Flora placed her hand upon it. "You are right, they are going to need more help. It is time for me to leave this cave and complete my destiny so that the legacy can live on. *Please, please* let there be enough inside me to see this through."

CHAPTER 19

The Hungry Tree

There is no way I am going to even try to figure out how Flora did that!" Dylan declared as he and Joelle found themselves immediately in the middle of the forest.

"Did you hear what she said before we left?" Joelle asked.

"Something about doors. There are a lot of them around here. Look at them! They are scattered all over the place! This is so unbelievable!" Pulling Joelle with him, Dylan approached one of the doors directly in front of them.

"Actually, I can believe anything at this point. And Dylan? You can let go of my hand now."

"Huh?"

Raising their joined hands in front of Dylan's face, Joelle waited.

"Oh! Sure, sorry." Immediately after releasing Joelle's hand, Dylan stuffed both of his hands in his jean pockets.

"Do you think she meant for us to go through one of these doors? Maybe Maddie is in one of them with Modie," said Joelle.

"Only one way to find out." Taking hold of the black knob, Dylan turned it and pushed the door in.

With Joelle following close behind, Dylan led the way through the doorway. As soon as they cleared the entrance, the door disappeared and they found themselves in a beautiful grassy field. In front of them was a weeping willow tree with long graceful branches that begged someone to climb.

"Look at the tree. Maddie would love to climb it. She would be there in an instant," declared Dylan.

"*Who* would want to climb that tree?" asked Joelle.

"Ummm, I can't remember. What were we just talking about?" Rubbing his forehead, Dylan was feeling a bit confused.

"Doesn't matter, probably not important. Let's just stay here for a while," said Joelle.

About 20 yards away from the tree sat an ancient stone bench adorned with scrolled carvings. Together they walked around the tree and headed for the bench—drawn to it for some unknown reason. As they sat upon the cold hard surface, they watched as magnificent tulips immediately sprouted before their eyes. Tulips, in bright colors, filled the area.

"I don't understand this, Dylan. What were we supposed to do? I can't even seem to remember. All I want to do is stay right here on this bench and watch these flowers grow." Joelle gazed at the flowers as if she had never seen tulips before.

"Whatever we were supposed to do can't be as important as seeing this!" Dylan said in awe as he reached down picking several of the blossoming beauties and handing them to Joelle.

"Thank you, Dylan. No one has ever given me flowers before."

Smiling, Dylan thought maybe he should say something poetic but a rustling sound from behind them distracted him. He looked over his shoulder and called out, "Hey, is anyone there?"

"What's wrong?"

Frowning, Dylan looked at Joelle, "Nothing, I guess. I just thought I heard something. Did you?"

"No, not a thing." Another noise echoed. "Okay, I heard that." Joelle turned around and saw a black crow fly from the tree.

"Dylan! It was just a crow. Hey, wasn't that tree a little more over to the left? I could swear that we walked around it."

Dylan glanced back and noted the change in the tree's position. "This is getting too creepy. You are right! It was over there. At least I think it was."

"Dylan, trees do not just get up and move, do they? I mean, I know that there have been some weird things going on that we have experienced but I don't think that a tree moving around is a good thing."

The ground vibrated beneath their feet causing them to sit up straight, eyes wide and hearts pounding. Then they heard a heavy groan and more movement this time directly behind them.

Tiny green leaves floated in the air before their faces, landing softly in their laps. The sky turned dark with blue clouds rapidly rolling in. Thunder could be heard in the distance. All the beautiful tulips they were just admiring, along with the bouquet Joelle still clutched in one hand, were turning into lifeless stems. There was a feeling of dread around.

"Dylan, you can hold my hand again now," said the shaken Joelle. Dylan held Joelle's hand and softly squeezed it in reassurance. "Joelle, everything is fine. It is just a storm rolling in. The flowers probably died because well— just because—And it is completely impossible for that tree to be moving."

"Why don't you turn around and see?" Joelle asked.

"Why don't *you* turn around?"

"No way! I asked *you* first, so *you* do it."

"Okay, tell you what. We will do it together. On the count of three. One-two-three!"

Together they turned their heads only to encounter dark-brown bark. The weeping willow tree was literally bending over them as a large gaping hole opened in the center of the tree trunk.

Dylan and Joelle screamed and tried to leap off the bench only to find that they were held secure by stone fingers that were wrapped around their legs. The bench was holding them hostage!

Long finger-like branches, hunched forward with a deep groan, pushed their bodies towards the chasm in its trunk. The black void opened wider and the two adolescents got shoved in.

With arms wrapped around each other, Dylan and Joelle went spiraling down a tunnel. Their bodies slipped and slid on what seemed like a roller-coaster ride. A blue light opened before them as they went skidding through, landing with a jarring thud and knocking the breath out of them for a brief moment.

Wiping Joelle's hair out of her face, Dylan frantically search her face. "Joelle! Joelle! Are you all right?"

"Dylan? What happened? Where are we?" Pulling herself up on her elbows, Joelle looked around.

"JAKE!" She suddenly exclaimed. Scrambling over on all fours, she enveloped her brother in a hug.

"Hi guys. Don't tell me, a tree ate you, too?" Joelle's twin asked dryly.

Dylan clasped his best friend's hand and shook it. "Jake! Am I glad to see you! Have you seen Maddie?"

"Sorry, I haven't seen her. I pretty much have been here this whole time," Jake responded.

Dylan looked around, "Where on earth are we? And what is this thing we are in?"

"More like under earth and this thing is a cage." Jake, noticing his friend heading to the blue bars, stopped him before touching it. "Don't even try! These bars seem to be electrically charged somehow. See that stick over there?" Pointing towards a table, Jake continued, "It has some kind of power source coming from the crystal on its tip. It is controlling the cage surrounding us. A crow has been standing watch since I arrived but he left shortly before you got here."

"How did you get here?" Joelle asked.

"Same way you guys did, through that creepy, crawly tree. Seems that this place is a laboratory of some kind."

"Bravo! Bravo!" A slow clapping sound echoed in the cavern. "How impressive you meddling kids are," a sarcastic voice said. Exiting the shadows, Rasoz appeared.

"If it isn't Miss Rah-Rah and her sidekick boyfriend, Dylan. Tell me, how did you like that playroom with my tree?"

"Rasoz!" Dylan and Joelle called out together.

"Another point scored for the opposition. You have been educated well, I see. Must have been our weakening Flora who spilled all to you two."

"Who on earth is that?" asked Jake.

"He isn't of earth exactly, Jake. He is a banished Pilutar. The legends are true! The BellKeepers, Flora the Oracle. All of it." And pointing to the grinning Rasoz, "He is here to destroy everything in his path." Joelle explained to her brother.

"How eloquently put, Miss Rah-Rah."

"My name is Joelle, you freak!"

"Where is my sister, Rasoz?"

"Charming! The heartsick boyfriend can speak. I don't suppose you are talking about that little girl who is quite irritating? She will be along shortly with that Pilutar, Modie. Then I can deal with you all once and forever."

Noir's cawing could be heard, coming closer to the chamber. As soon as he saw Rasoz, he flew over and landed on his shoulder. A series of sounds came from the black bird and Rasoz listened with a wicked smile forming on his face.

"Well, it seems that they could be here sooner than we thought. Modie and Maddie are leaving one of Flora's doors as we speak. So, I must leave you for now but I will be back with company!"

"You keep your hands off my sister!" yelled Dylan as he charged the blue bars. As soon as his body connected, he was zapped with an electric shock just enough to stop him from trying again.

Rasoz's laugh, so filled with evil and hate, vibrated and echoed as he made his way through the tunnel towards the forest.

CHAPTER 20

The Black Knob

M*odie!* You were going to save me from the gangplank, right?" Maddie asked Modie again as he shut the play-room door.

"Maddie, it was just a game. I keep telling you that."

"I know and I will keep asking until you answer me. These rooms of yours aren't fun for me, you know. I get to pick the next one, hey! What happened to your arm?" Maddie took Modie's arm and turned it into the sunlight to get a better look. "You are missing some of your fur!"

"It must have happened in the playroom," Modie responded and proceeded to take off Maddie's ball cap briefly to rub the top of his head.

"Do you have another headache? You know, this happened to my granddad. He lost his hair, too. He said it was from stress. That would even explain your headaches. Can I have my cap back now?"

"Nope, I am going to keep it for a while. I like it. Makes me feel like I am grown up like my dad. He wears a cap too. Not like yours though." Settling the ball cap back on his head,

Modie started towards the mountain. "Come on, Maddie. Maybe this time we will reach Bellmaur Peak before Rasoz gets near us. We need to get to that clearing just ahead. Once we get through the entrance we will be able to get my dad's BellKey."

Just before they reached the mountain Modie's BellKey rang.

GONG! GONG! GONG!

Seeing two doors near them, Modie ran for one, yelling at Maddie to follow him. With his hand on the gold knob, he turned to make sure that Maddie was there. She wasn't.

Maddie was standing by the other door.

"No way, Modie! I get to pick the next door and we are going through this one!"

GONG! GONG! GONG! GONG!

"Better hurry, Modie. Rasoz is really close now."

"Fine! We will go through your door. Just get it opened and fast!"

Maddie took the black knob and turned it. Together they went through the door that she had chosen.

Once inside, the two were surrounded with sights and sounds of a county fair. A beautiful carousel slowly spun with the overly decorated horses going up and down. Organs played classical music that beckoned the children to come and ride.

"Now *this* is what I call a playroom! We even have cotton candy and most of all I am NOT wearing a frilly dress. I still have on my jeans." Maddie declared her triumph as she skipped towards the carousel that had stopped. "Let's ride this, Modie. Then we can try out the ferris wheel and the games. Are you any good at throwing balls? Maybe you can win me a stuffed animal." Maddie climbed onboard the ride and wandered around the circle platform until she found a white horse with a blue decorated saddle.

"Maddie, where are the other people? In my playrooms there were always others to play with," Modie asked as he followed her and picked a brown horse with a red saddle.

"This is *my* playroom, Modie, that's why." Biting off a glob of cotton candy, she mumbled to her friend, "Remember, hold the pole tight. Sometimes when these rides start, you jerk some."

On cue the ride started with their horses gradually moving up and down. Slowly the carousel spun progressively picking up speed. Maddie's blonde curls flew about her face making her laugh. Modie's face broke into a grin and he decided that this wasn't too bad after all. Laughing, they both threw their cotton candy in the air and held on to the pole with both hands.

GONG! GONG!

"What? Why is your BellKey ringing like that?" Maddie asked.

"This is impossible, Maddie. Rasoz can't be in here. Flora said we were safe in the playrooms."

The carousel picked up speed.

GONG! GONG!

Faster they spun.

"Modie, I am getting dizzy! Can't you make it stop?"

"I can't, Maddie, I can't," Modie yelled out.

The poles connecting to the carousel horses broke off. The horses' heads whipped around and black eyes stared at the two children who rode them.

"They are coming alive!" Maddie screamed. "Talk to them, Modie! Make them stop!"

"They aren't listening! I have already tried!"

Saddle straps appeared and wrapped around Modie and Maddie, securing them in place.

The horses went wild, leaping off the carousel platform keeping their hostages firmly placed on their backs. There was nothing that they could do but wrap their arms around the stallions' necks and hold on tight.

Both horses raced through a single door, bringing the children back into the forest, to the waiting Rasoz who stood at the entrance of Bellmaur Peak.

"Well, isn't this special?" Rasoz said with false humor as he wiped a fake tear from his eye. "My little Pilutar has come back to the fold."

"Let us go Rasoz. You will not win. I will see to that." From the horse's back, Modie glared down at his enemy.

"Oh, please! I have already accomplished what I set out to do. I have you, Modie, and soon you will do as I ask."

"I am not yours to control, Rasoz. Your time is very limited. Flora knows about you."

Laughing, Rasoz walked closer to Modie's horse. "You are so droll, child. My, how I have missed you! Have you missed me? And haven't we grown up since I last saw you. I see that you are losing some of your fur covering. Leaving the Seed Cycle, are you?"

"That is stress!" Maddie shouted.

Ignoring Modie's little friend, Rasoz continued, "I feel responsible for you now, Modie. What with your parents abandoning you and all. Tell me, how did you like *my* playroom?"

"*Your* playroom?" Modie asked as he struggled against the straps still holding him.

"Of course, mine! Did you not think that I would figure out that little scheme of Flora's? I just made my own playrooms.

It really was only a matter of time before you went into one. Of course, they have been quite popular lately with other members of the LaHiere Village. Do the names Dylan, Joelle and Jake mean anything to you, dear Maddie?"

"Where are they? What have you done to them?" cried out Maddie.

"Maddie, what is it?" Modie saw that she was getting upset. "Who are they?"

"Dylan is my big brother, Modie. Jake and Joelle are his friends. Rasoz must have them!"

"True, how true. They are my insurance that you will do as I say." He turned his attention to the horses and said, "Release them and be on your way."

The straps loosened around their captives. Modie and Maddie slid off the horses. With a snap of his fingers, Rasoz sent the horses galloping into the forest, disappearing from sight.

"Don't even think about trying any tricks, *Mighty Modie*. You two will follow me back into my chambers. Then we will have a discussion about the whereabouts of your father's BellKey and then you will turn over *your* BellKey to me."

"And if I won't?" Modie asked with his chin held high.

"Then three teenagers will pay the price along with your little friend here." Rasoz reached out and grabbed both children by their upper arms and started to walk into the mountain, dragging them with him.

Once they were inside the mountain, Modie looked up and noted the familiar presence of General Alucard and his troops.

"We are standing by, sir," said the very loyal General Alucard.

"Stand down this time, Alu. Rasoz is already on to you and the men. This mission is something that I will have to go through without your backup." He put his hand to his forehead and quickly saluted his friend.

"What are you doing? I told you no tricks!" Rasoz declared as he saw Modie move his hand.

"He has a headache and it is probably because of you. Stress does that to a person, you know," Maddie snapped.

"You are quite mouthy, child. That is something that will not be tolerated." Rasoz continued to lead the children down the left tunnel.

"Modie, what are we going to do?" Maddie looked behind Rasoz's back as she stumbled along next to the banished Ancient One.

"Have faith, Maddie. Just follow my lead and do as I ask. Can you do that for me?"

"You are talking to me in my head again. I really wish I knew how we do this!" *"Somehow, we have always been connected, Maddie, please just do as I say."*

"Okay, just as long as I don't have to wear frilly dresses!"

"That's what I wanted to hear." Smiling Modie looked at Maddie and winked.

"You two are awfully quiet." Rasoz observed suspiciously.

"Just following you, Rasoz. Just like you wanted," Modie reassured him. "We are not going to give you any problems. Are we Maddie?"

"Nope, no problems at all."

"Hmmm, why don't I believe you?" Seeing the Dead End wall ahead, Rasoz stopped. "I am going to go through with irritating Miss Maddie first. You will then immediately follow, Modie. Understood?"

"Completely," with a nod of his head Modie acknowledged him.

"Modie, there is a wall in front of us!"

"Trust me, Maddie."

Rasoz let go of Modie and pulled Maddie through the Dead

End wall. As she went through, she watched Modie who slightly smiled, *"It is okay!"*

As soon as Modie saw that they were clear of the wall, he entered. He paused and reached down searching for the Bell-Key he hid there earlier.

Come on, come on—it has to be here somewhere! Feeling the solid gold BellKey, his hand immediately grasped it. As he finished going through the wall, he hid his hand behind his back. He walked directly in front of Maddie and made sure that she noticed what he had hidden in his hand.

"OH!" Maddie gasped out loud.

Rasoz gave her a sharp look. "What, what is it?"

"Ah, nothing! Just feeling weird from walking through a wall."

"You are doing great, Maddie. Now, take my dad's BellKey and put it in your pocket. Quickly! Do it NOW!"

Without Rasoz noticing, Maddie did as Modie asked. The BellKey that was so coveted was now safe in her jeans pocket.

CHAPTER 21

Modie's Plan

"Dylan!" He struggled against Rasoz's hold, and Maddie tried to break free.

"Go, go have your sappy reunion with your brother and his friends but stay by the cage." He released his hold on Maddie's shoulder and gave her a push. "Modie and I still have a discussion to conduct." He pulled Modie closer to his body and he bent down and whispered, "As you can see, I do have the insurance that you will do as I say."

Modie watched his friend race over to where the teenagers were held secure and he then took in the situation.

Noir was perched on the table where Rasoz's staff rested. The beam projected from the crystal contained Maddie's brother and friends. Rasoz still stood where they came in, so that exit was blocked. There was still his tunnel that he made previously, but only Maddie and he could fit through it. It was way too small for the others. There has to be another way out for them! But where?

Modie looked over the entire area once again, and he started to form a plan in his mind.

"Maddie, are you all right?" Dylan asked as she got closer to the cage.

"I'm okay."

"Who is that fur ball creature with the red eyes, Maddie?"

"Modie is not a fur ball, he is my best friend. He will get us out of here. You will see." Maddie went to touch the glowing bars but Joelle stopped her.

"Don't touch them, Maddie. You will get zapped."

"We are completely trapped in here. How will Modie help us? You can't tell me he can help. He is no bigger than you, Maddie." Despite Maddie's assurances, Jake was skeptical about Modie's ability to get them out of there. "Just free us out of this thing and I will show him who he is messing with!"

"He will help. Knowing Modie, it could be anything. Just be ready." Turning, Maddie faced Modie who was slowly moving away from Rasoz.

"It is time, little Pilutar. You know what I want. Tell me where your father's BellKey is or they will suffer." Rasoz nodded at Noir who used one of his talons and rotated the staff. The blue beam shined brighter and the cage shrunk.

Gasping, Joelle clung to the two boys as the cage came closer to her skin. The three huddled together and looked at Maddie who still stood patiently outside the cage.

"It's okay. We have to trust Modie," she whispered to them.

"The BellKey really is not far from you now," said Modie, who edged a bit away from Rasoz and did some calculations.

"Maddie, get ready. I want you to throw the BellKey up in the air when I say so."

Putting her hand in her pocket, Maddie felt her palm connect with the cool gold. *"Ready."*

"You know, Rasoz, my father's BellKey is just one of three. Even if I gave you mine and you had the two BellKeys, you will never have my mother's. She has that BellKey with her. So, what good are they to you?" Running a finger across the table that he now stood by, Modie glanced at Rasoz's staff from the corner of his eye.

Noir crowed his displeasure that Modie was so close to him.

Rasoz eyed Modie, speculating on the wisdom of telling the Pilutar his plan. "I suppose it wouldn't hurt to tell you my scheme." His black eyes gleamed and antennae twitched. "The BellKeys have great power, as you well know, Pilutar. The destruction I can create is unimaginable if I have all three. Since that is not possible, I can deal with having just two. With the two BellKeys I can join their magic with my crystal that I, well, let's just say that I have great plans to destroy the Kingdom of Enchantment. You are already living in a part of my plan. So easily you are deceived!"

"You are sick!" declared Jake.

"Not sick, ruthless. Sounds better, don't you agree?"

"I have another question," Modie said.

"Last one, *Mighty Modie.* I am getting weary of this stalling." Faking a yawn, Rasoz looked at Modie.

"You were banished by Flora. Once someone is sent through the Banishing Door they are not supposed to be able to get out. How did you?"

Rasoz laughed and took great pleasure in telling. "Sent through the Banishing Door? My, my . . . so, your Oracle has kept the secret. She did not even trust her beloved Bell-Keepers . . . interesting."

"Modie . . . ?" Maddie asked with a puzzled expression. "A secret?"

Modie just shook his head. He did not know what Rasoz was talking about either.

"Just ignore him, Maddie. He will say anything to sway for faith."

"Faith? In Flora?" Snickering, Rasoz looked over at Maddie and then back to Modie—deciding what to say. Should he give away Flora . . . or wait? Time was ticking away but in his favor.

"I will tell you this . . . the Skylar Realm underestimated the power of their gifts. I, of course, appreciated all that they could offer me! So, I used their gifts to my advantage . . . my favorite one of all . . . earthquakes . . . the force that was the key to opening the Door. Now, enough already with these questions. I am bored. The BellKey, where is it?"

"Actually, Rasoz, the BellKey is right in this room," revealed Modie as he turned Maddie's lucky ball cap backwards on his head.

"What? Where? Where is the BellKey? Give it to me!" Rasoz looked around him frantically. He took a step forward towards Modie, reaching out his hand. Again he demanded, "I want that BellKey and I want it NOW!"

"NOW MADDIE!" Modie yelled.

Maddie flung her hand up into the air and the BellKey soared with the gold glinting as it spun in circles. The magical object sensed that one of its mates was near and sent out a musical call.

Modie's BellKey answered as he leaped up. The Bells joined forming two thirds of its symbol. Completing his flight with a somersault, Modie landed on Zosar's staff. The scepter shot up causing the blue beam to retract—freeing the teenagers.

Grabbing the evil weapon, Modie pointed it to the rocky ceiling above Rasoz. The power shot free and the earth's formation crumbled down burying his arch enemy. Noir flew to where his master was entombed and frantically pecked at the rocks.

"I just knew you could do it, Modie!" Maddie ran over to her friend and hugged him causing Modie to drop the Rasoz's staff.

A look of dismay showed on her face when she felt his arm. "Oh, no Modie! You are losing more fur. Your whole arm is bare!"

"Don't worry about that right now, Maddie. We have to get out of here."

"Yeah and our only exit is blocked." Jake said as he pointed to where Rasoz was covered in rumble.

"It will be okay. Modie has a plan. He always has a plan. He got us this far didn't he?" Leaning closer to Modie, she whispered to him, "You do have a plan, right?"

"*Mighty Modie, the wall still blocks the water.*" General Alucard's voice entered Modie's mind.

"Yes, I have a plan but someone may not like it."

"Someone? Do you mean me? I don't like that look you have, Modie. It reminds me of when we were in the pirate playroom. What are you planning? You better tell me and tell me now."

Modie shook his head and stepped aside from the group. All his focus went to the area where he had once created the dam to close off the access to the LaHiere River. He waved one arm and his gift was then reversed. Slabs of rocks and boulders lifted from the ground and re-established themselves back in their original positions. Swirling water came rushing through and filled the cavern pool as it once was before.

Modie pointed to the water. "You will need to jump in there and swim out of the cavern. It really is no more than 15 yards of under-water swimming. As soon as you are clear of the cavern, you just swim to the surface of the LaHiere River and climb up the bank that leads you to the meadow. There you will be safe."

"What about Maddie? She can't swim," Dylan asked.

"I am not too keen on swimming in the dark either, Modie," Joelle replied.

Dylan and Joelle looked at Jake who just shrugged his shoulders. "What? I can swim this."

Soon all three teenagers were talking at once with Maddie putting in her two cents.

Holding his hand up, Modie commanded silence.

"We are running out of time! You three HAVE to go in the water. There is no other way. Maddie and I are going to take my escape tunnel. It is way too small for anyone else to go through." As he rubbed the ball cap on top his head in what seemed like frustration, Modie heard the rocks moving over Rasoz's form.

"GO! GO! We are out of time." Modie ordered.

Jake jumped into the water first with Joelle following. Dylan watched their forms disappear before turning to his sister. "Please tell me you will get out fast. I am already going to have a time explaining all of this to mom and dad."

"I will! I promise. Modie will be with me the whole time."

Pointing his finger at Modie, Dylan ordered, "And you! You better get my sister out of here safely. I am counting on you."

"You have my word, Dylan, brother to my best friend."

With a final look at his sister, who smiled reassuringly at him, Dylan jumped into the water.

More of the rocks surrounding Rasoz tumbled free. A single arm broke through and began to claw at the surrounding rubble.

"He is coming out! He is coming out! Let's go Modie! Come on!" Tugging on Modie's arm, Maddie tried to pull him to the exit tunnel.

Again Modie was shaking his head.

"What? What are you waiting for? Why do you have that look back on your face?" Maddie desperately gazed at Modie.

"No, no!" She shook her head side to side in denial, after

she realized what Modie had planned all along. Maddie looked at her best friend. "But I can't swim."

"Rasoz is breaking free, Maddie. We will never make it through my tunnel. We have to go into the water." Taking his dearest friend's hand, Modie gazed straight into her eyes.

"Maddie, you have to trust me. I will save you! Do you hear me? I would have saved you in the pirate playroom and *I WILL SAVE YOU NOW!*"

Coughing and sputtering, Rasoz pulled his upper body up. Seeing Noir, he bellowed, "NOIR! GET ME MY STAFF!"

"No more time, Maddie. This is it. Hold your breath and close your eyes. I will not let go of you!"

"I better get a BellKey after this!" Maddie took a deep breath and with her eyes scrunched close, she grabbed hold of Modie's hand. With her other hand she plugged her nose and plunged into the unknown.

CHAPTER 22

Modie Keeps His Promise

You are doing great, Maddie. Hang in there!" Still holding on to
Maddie's hand, Modie navigated the cavern's cold, ink-
black water, kicking his feet rapidly to propel them. He knew
that talking to Maddie with his mind kept her reassured, so
Modie continued, *"We are just about through the cavern."*

Modie was feeling his strength weakening from pulling
Maddie's weight plus his own. He knew that he would need
help in order to keep his promise. He took his mind from his
friend for a brief moment to call upon the Skylar Realm for
their assistance on the surface and then sought out the help
of a school of salmon.

The fish came to his aid by settling themselves underneath
Maddie like a bed. Gently they swam to the surface bringing Maddie up with them. As they broke through the water,
a wind storm sent by the Skylar Realm picked up the child.
Spiraling in protection around Maddie's small body, the wind
storm shifted and brought her gently to the meadow where
her brother and parents were waiting.

Maddie's eyes fluttered open to the sight of her parents

leaning over her with looks of concern on their faces. Dylan was off to the side with Joelle and Jake who were slightly shivering in the cool evening air.

With the help of her parents, Maddie got up. "I made it? I made it! I just knew I could swim! Modie saved me, Mom and Dad! He saved me just like he promised. Granddad's story about the BellKeepers was true, you know."

Throngs of people from the LaHiere Village pushed forward to see Maddie. In the center of them all was Flora.

"Excuse me, excuse me, coming through! How about a little crowd control here, people." Flora moved everyone aside to get to Maddie. She saw the young girl that she had secretly watched the past ten years grinning at her parents and that brought a smile to her face.

"My, my! You have recovered nicely!" Flora praised.

"Oh! You must be Flora!" Maddie walked over to the woman she had heard so much about from Modie and gave her a hug. The hug that Flora, for ten years, had been waiting for.

"What are you doing out of your cave? I thought you weren't supposed to leave it. Oh! I loved the playrooms. Well, except for the pirate one. But Modie made up for that because he saved me this time."

"Where is Modie, child?"

"Why, I don't know. Wasn't he right behind me?" Maddie looked around. She asked her parents and others about Modie.

"DYLAN!" Seeing her brother talking to Jake and Joelle, Maddie cried out." Where is Modie?"

"He must still be in the river!" Dylan, Jake and Joelle raced to the water's edge with Flora following.

Jake was the first to see Modie slowly pulling himself out of the water. "There he is!"

Flora stopped them from going down to the edge. "I will

take care of Modie. Please go back to your families. I need you to organize everyone. Ask them to stand back away from the gold wall. We still need to get Modie's parents back and need the room to do so."

Dylan and Jake went back to do as Flora asked while she reached down and grasped Modie's hand.

Flora pulled him up and wrapped her arms around Modie, silently giving thanks for his safety.

"Flora! What are you doing here?" Modie asked with a very weak voice.

"I knew that help would be needed so I went into the village and sought it. People came from all over that town just to see that you and the others were safe."

"You left your cave, for me?"

"It was time, Modie. All that has come to pass was meant to be." Flora reached up and took off the ball cap that still sat securely on Modie's head. With a bright smile on her face, Flora exclaimed, "Just look at you! My, how you have grown! You are entering the Bud Cycle, dear child. You are growing antennae!"

Modie put a hand on top of his head and felt around. Sure enough! He could feel the two knobs forming on the top of his skull.

"This is why my head has been hurting! Maddie thought it was stress." In afterthought he yelled, "Maddie! Where is she? Is she all right?" Putting the cap back on his head, Modie looked around.

Pointing up ahead, Flora showed Modie. "See, your adorable Maddie is with her family along with her brother. Jake and Joelle are safe, too! I am so very, very proud of you, Mighty Modie!"

"Thanks, Flora," said Modie, who felt good that everyone

was safe but sad after seeing everyone reunited with their families.

Flora, too, though thankful that everything turned out all right, was uneasy. "Come, Modie. It is time to bring back your parents. We still are not through."

Scrambling up the embankment, Flora and Modie walked hand in hand into the meadow. When the crowd of people from LaHiere Village saw the pair, they were delighted. A resounding cheer filled the air.

Together, Flora and Modie continued towards the golden wall. When they reached the wall, Flora gently slipped off the two joining BellKeys from around his neck.

"You may have the honor, Modie."

With a hopeful grin, Modie took hold of the BellKeys and threw them into the golden wall, which absorbed the treasure.

Suddenly, there was a dazzling display of colorful lights emitting from the barrier as it renounced its presence. The Royal Draugs disappeared and in their place were Modie's parents and the three joined BellKeys hovering—leading the way. In recognition of the BellKeepers' presence, the meadow immediately became a thriving area. Green grass sprouted, hundreds of bright, colorful tulips blossomed.

Modie ran the short distance to his parents, feeling their arms wrap around his now maturing body. The crowd, happy at their reunion, cheered.

"Son, we are so proud of you!" Jamar knelt down to Modie's level. "You have made some tough choices but by following your heart and beliefs, the faith in the Pilutars will now be reestablished."

"Oh, Modie! Just look at you." Ashlar, her hands over his arms, feeling the missing fur.

"I'm growing antennae, Mom!" Modie declared proudly as

he took off the ball cap to show his mom and then promptly put it back on.

"Yes, son. You are! A sign of a true young man who has earned the right."

A crack of thunder reverberated from the forest. The sound reminded all of the anger that was felt by the one who portrayed it.

The three Bellkeepers walked toward the forest and watched as the sky turned dark and forbidding. Blue lightning bolts traveled and spread toward the meadow. Townspeople whispered their concern.

"Rasoz!" Modie looked at his parents. "I wasn't able to stop him. I saw him take some of your BellKey's power, Dad! He is more powerful now."

Jamar placed his hand on his son's shoulder and said, "We will take care of Rasoz, together, as the three BellKeepers."

Townspeople scattered into small huddles as Modie and his parents moved back into the middle of the meadow. The formidable and unified BellKey stood guard in front as they turned and waited for Rasoz the Banished One.

Residents of LaHiere Village called out their support for they knew that whatever had been occurring in their forest needed to come to an end. They also realized the legends that had been told to them from ancestors about the Pilutars were true. The legend of the BellKeepers was coming alive right before them.

A thick blue cloud tumbled towards the meadow. Sharp lightning bolts slashed and exploded. A foggy mist seeped and slithered from the forest ground, blanketing the meadow's grass. Rasoz's shadow appeared and came forward with the staff in his hand. With his battered monk-like robe flowing and eyes devoid of feeling, Rasoz completed his grand entrance.

A hushed silence fell on the meadow. The only sound heard was from Noir, who was perched on Rasoz's shoulder, cawing his resentment.

Rasoz belligerently faced the BellKeepers. His lip curled in disgust when he saw the joined symbol hanging in the air. "I see you managed to complete the BellKey after all, *Mighty Modie*. But, you never managed to defeat ME!" He turned his attention to the crowd in the background and roared as he spun his staff in the air, "You simple mortals! Watch and learn. For when I have overcome your cherished BellKeepers, you will be next. I will control—"

Flora's voice stopped his tirade.

"You will not control anything, Rasoz. You are going to have to go through me first."

A sickening laugh erupted from Rasoz. "Came out of your exile, Flora? How quaint and apropos. You think you are a threat to me? Just look at you! You are an old woman now whose magic is lost."

Flora stood proudly in front of her BellKeepers with her arms held wide. The hovering completed—Bellkey stayed close to her shoulder. Her gray braided hair hung limp down the front of her rounded body. The tiny bell around her neck flashed then dimmed while her antennae drooped in response.

"Flora! What are you doing? Let us handle Rasoz!" Jamar demanded.

Without turning around and keeping her gaze steady on her archrival, Flora calmly spoke, "This is my battle. For I am the one who originally banished Rasoz. This is how it should be."

The earth vibrated as Rasoz slammed his staff's end down on the ground. "Yes, it is your battle. They must not find out the secret, now should they Flora?" Rasoz said with a sneer. "Let's finish it!" he growled.

Whipping his scepter straight, the crystal glowed shooting a beam directly at Flora, enveloping and lifting her up into the air. With a twist of his wrist, the emission of light turned a brighter blue and Flora's body bent back in response, too weak to even grab the almighty BellKey contained in her.

Townspeople were dismayed. Ashlar and Jamar immediately went forward to assist Flora but Modie stopped them.

"She needs to do this. I think she always knew that she would be the one."

"Look at your beloved Oracle now! She does not even have the strength or power to win!" Laughing in victory Rasoz brought the beam higher in the air.

"No strength or power—she needs magic," Modie thought. A glimmer of hope entered his heart as he realized that all was not lost.

"Maddie! Maddie!" Modie called out to her with his thoughts. *"Have everyone circle the meadow. They need to join hands and send their beliefs to Flora."*

"I hear you, Modie."

"Hurry! Hurry! She does not have much time."

At Maddie's bidding, the people of LaHiere Village quickly joined hands with Modie and his parents standing in the front. In a united force, faith and love filled their hearts and minds feeding the Natural Earth who in turn sent it to the once Oracle of the Pilutars.

Flora's antennae received the offering from the Natural Earth and fed her suffering body. Strength poured into her veins. Her antennae straightened with her body. Her sudden burst of energy had her whipping her head up proudly and her eyes glowing in a translucent blue.

The Pilutar power shimmered around her as her gray hair gradually turned to white. The braid unwound and flowed freely; her old, rounded body became young and vibrant. Flora, Oracle of the Pilutars, was reborn.

"What was it you lectured to Modie, Rasoz?" Flora asked as she reached for the BellKey by her shoulder, "Ah, yes! Always look beyond the surface!"

"No! This can't be! It is not possible!" Rasoz roared and Noir screeched, his wings flapping in the air and took off in flight over the meadow.

With her now young hands, wrapped around the BellKey, Flora bowed her head. The blue sphere around her gradually turned gold defying the evil force that contained her. The circle descended and as her delicate, bare feet touched the ground, she pushed her hands forward sending the BellKey's energy towards Rasoz.

Golden power shot out exploding the staff from Rasoz's grip, shattering the crystal into pieces. Flora let go of the BellKey sending it back to Modie and his parents.

Rasoz saw the crystal shards falling to the ground and reached for one holding it between two fingers. "You have no idea what you have just done! This is not over!" With a sick grin on his face, Rasoz flicked the shard towards Flora.

"But, it is Rasoz." And with all the energy left in her bell, Flora sharply whipped her head up in the air and focused on a single point. The dreaded brown Door appeared in the horizon. The last of the Royal Draugs in her care soared up to the door and opened it.

The Door's vortex power transferred onto Rasoz. As his body was sucked back into his prison, Rasoz yelled out for all to hear.

"I will achieve my goal. This is only the beginning!" Rasoz's voice echoed.

When the Door closed and disappeared from sight, Flora

collapsed to the ground. Her own dainty bell around her neck glowed bright then became dull and lifeless as her antennae vanished from sight. There lying on the ground was a young woman who is now mortal because she sacrificed everything to save the ones she loved just as her father, The Regent, had done before.

Epilogue — Destined To Be

Though the townspeople of LaHiere Village wanted to cheer and celebrate, their concern for Flora took precedence. Everyone tried to get a glimpse of the prone figure.

Jamar and Ashlar held everyone back as Modie and Maddie went to sit by Flora's side.

"Flora! Wake up now, you can do it," beseeched Modie as he patted her hand.

"Modie, look how beautiful she is!" Maddie looked at her in wonder.

Groaning, Flora sat up and looked around her. "I refuse to be silly and say, *what happened.*"

"You did it, Flora! You did save us!" Modie declared. "I so glad that this is all over with."

"Perhaps it is just beginning for you, Modie." Flora mysteriously replied.

"But, why give up your gifts, Flora?" questioned Maddie "I just don't understand that at all."

"It was by my choice, Maddie. I have so enjoyed watching the human race grow and wishing that I could be a part of that. Now, I can be."

Flora reached down and pulled the two children to their feet.

"Modie! Your bravery needs to be rewarded. I have gifted you with my ability to create doors. You can now have your own playrooms."

"Thank you, Flora!"

"It is now time for Modie and his family to go back to the Pilutar Realm. There, questions will need to be answered and discussed." Seeing Maddie's look of dismay, Flora reassured her. "All will be as it is meant to be, child. I am going to stay and live here in the LaHiere Village to be near you."

Jamar and Ashlar used the joined BellKey to call on the Veil of Sanctuary. The entrance door appeared and waited for them to enter. Patiently, they stood to the side so Modie could say his good-byes to Maddie.

"You are the bestest friend ever, Modie!" Wrapping her little arms around Modie's neck, Maddie held tight. "I am going to miss you!"

Trying so hard to be brave and strong, Modie, too, put his arms around his friend. "I will miss you, too, Maddie!"

Maddie touched the ball cap on top of Modie's head and smiled. "You can keep my hat to remember me by."

"But, I don't have anything to give you."

"Of course, you do Modie." Flora approached the pair as she took off her bell necklace from around her neck. "You can give her my bell. It is of no use to me now." Smiling, Flora handed Modie the necklace.

Gently, Modie put the ornament over Maddie's head. As it went around her neck and nestled against her body, the bell flickered. "This may not be a BellKey, but it is the next best thing."

Maddie softly kissed him on the cheek. "Thank you, Modie. I will cherish it forever."

Slightly embarrassed, Modie walked over to where his parents were waiting. Together the three BellKeepers went through to the Veil of Sanctuary one by one.

With one foot in the door, Modie turned the ball cap around backwards on his head and waved good-bye to the cheering townspeople before closing the door that then faded from sight.

In the far corner of the meadow, a hidden figure watched as Flora and Maddie started to leave. Its shadow was cast upon the grass in a misshapen form. A hand picked a tulip from the meadow then crushed it within its menacing grip.

Startled, Maddie stopped walking and turned around looking back. A shudder racked her body and a feeling of uneasiness traveled her spine. Something was out there. She could feel it; just watching. Wrapping her arms around her middle, Maddie ducked her head feeling tears well up in her eyes.

"What? What is it, Maddie?"

"I don't know. For a second I felt like someone was watching me. It was strange, you know?"

Flora glanced at the meadow. She, too, felt like something was out there. The trees surrounding the meadow softly rustled from a slight breeze. Flora watched the movement before she noted that the color seemed a bit dim now that she was mortal.

"You will feel better after you have had some rest . . . we both will. You have gone through so much today with Modie." Flora stoked her hand down Maddie's hair in comfort.

Maddie looked up to Flora. "Modie," Maddie sighed. "Do you think I will ever see Modie again?"

The bell around the young child's neck glowed very bright in response.

Flora gave a knowing smile.